LOVE WITCH

TORRENT WITCHES COZY MYSTERIES
BOOK SEVEN

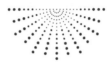

TESS LAKE

Shadow Witch

Torrent Witches Box Set #2 (Fabulous Witch, Holiday Witch, Shadow Witch)

Love Witch

Cozy Witch

Lost Witch

Wicked Witch

CHAPTER ONE

"*R*epeat that line," Hans fumed.

Anton quailed, which, if you know Anton, is *astounding*. The guy was a former Marine. I have two stories about him.

One: Anton is a hunter. Every year he goes up to Alaska and treks out into the snow with nothing more than a knife and a few supplies. He hand-makes a bow and arrow and then hunts. One year he stepped in a bear trap. It crushed his ankle and locked so he couldn't remove it. As he was dragging himself back to the nearest town (some twelve miles away), a bear attacked him, possibly drawn by the blood trail.

He fought off the bear. Killed it actually.

Four days later he makes it to town, turns up at the ER and *takes a seat* because there is a queue of people.

He waits, bear trap on his leg, quietly bleeding until eventually the staff notice and immediately rush him in for treatment.

Ask him about it and he says it wasn't a bad hunting trip. *Most* of it was pretty good.

Second story: Anton is doing some work on his home

1

when he slips off the ladder and crashes through the fence, impaling his leg. His wife comes home to find the paramedics loading him into the ambulance. There is a trail of blood leading from the fence, down to his workshop and back again. Blood all over his angle grinder. Why? *Because he knew he wouldn't be able to get in the ambulance with a whopping great metal spike through his leg, so he cut it off with his angle grinder before calling the ambulance.*

I spoke to one of the paramedics at the time, news-gathering, and she said he didn't cry, didn't call out in pain, didn't make a sound, not even when the spike jarred against the ambulance when they were loading him in.

The guy is made of stone covered by another layer of even *harder* stone.

"I... I... I..." Anton stammered.

Hans slapped him with a very well-worn copy of *The Taming of the Shrew*. In Anton's role as Baptista, the father of Katherine and Bianca, he was wearing an enormous prop nose. It tore off and went flying across the room, leaving Anton with strands of spirit gum stuck to his face.

"We open in three weeks! Everyone needs to be off book within the next two days, or I swear I'm going to kill you!" Hans roared.

Did I hate him? Oh, yes, indeed. Once again I was doing the sums in my mind: how much abuse could I take for the money I was making? I was starting to think uncomplicated poverty was looking *really* attractive right now.

I'd applied to work as a stage assistant for the Holtz Theatrical Company, not expecting I'd get it. To my surprise, I was hired. I'd met Esmeralda Huggins, the stage manager, and Hans' second-in-charge. Her last name was a clue to her nature: she was lovely and frequently handing out hugs.

I soon found out why she was required: Hans Holtz,

director and close to one of the worst, most rude people I'd ever met (and that's saying something).

He was a genius director, apparently, and in the last decade had pioneered a new concept. His traveling theater company would go to new towns and cities and draw from the locals to put on performances. He had a reputation as a perfectionist, a madman, and a brute.

He'd also discovered more new talent than virtually anyone. Teenagers plucked from obscurity by him were now movie stars. Every few years he'd do a Broadway production, and movie stars would be lining up for the smallest of roles.

Behind Hans, I saw Kira stone-faced, only the narrowing of her eyes betraying her thoughts. She was playing Katherine, the titular "shrew" and like many of the teenagers who were in the play hoped this would lead to much more.

I'd already had to warn her off cursing him. I hadn't enjoyed doing that because I was thinking of brewing up a curse myself. Something involving severe digestive distress, as a starter.

Somewhere from around the back of the set came the ominous tones of a piano. Marcus Fyfe, the music director, was warming up, oblivious to the drama happening out in front.

"I will. I am. I promise," Anton said.

He wiped away a tear.

Yes, that's right folks, a man who *fought and killed a bear* was crying because of the director.

"Oh my everyone, let's take a ten-minute break and then we'll try again!" Esmeralda said, bustling across the room.

"Broken legs is what they need!" Hans said and walked off. He turned in the doorway and pointed a finger at me.

"You, coffee, black and boiling in two minutes," he demanded.

Oh, you stuck-up arrogant piece of s-

3

"Be right there," I chirped.

He walked out, and I again imagined the satisfaction of throwing something at him.

How would I get his coffee to boiling point? Right now I could use a little of the fury bubbling away inside me.

Once again I considered that maybe Jack was right: no amount of money was worth this.

Although the money was good, it wasn't the only reason I was staying. Apart from not having anything else to do (having cut myself free from being a small-town journalist), I felt increasingly protective over the teenagers who were in the play. One teenager in particular - Kira.

She was strong and could be spiky, but she was also gentle and young. She definitely did not need some horrible man treating her badly just because no one had ever punched him in the face and told him to stop it.

(That wasn't *entirely* accurate. Hans had been stabbed once by an actor during an argument that broke out while rehearsing *A Midsummer Night's Dream*. But my point still stands: Hans hadn't learned *anything* from this.)

There was another reason: Jack and I had saved her from the Shadow Witch, and both of us felt an obligation to continue protecting her.

Kira had been distraught and angry (as you would be if an evil witch had tried to steal your body and kill you) and although she seemed to have bounced back, there were still times I saw a wariness in her, a sign that she wasn't okay.

The Shadow Witch had used Jack's body to grab Kira off the street. She'd then drugged me before taking us both to an underground room where she was going to perform the body-stealing ritual. She would have drained my life, almost to the point of death and then shoved Kira out of her body, to take it for her own.

We'd stopped her but it was a horrific thing, and I was sure Kira was still dealing with it.

I turned around, heading for the kitchen and Kira caught my eye. She pulled a face, sticking out her tongue and I couldn't help but smile.

Maybe things would be okay. It was only three more weeks. Others had survived Hans Holtz.

I went to the kitchen, passing by Anton who was surrounded by people telling him he was doing great, it's okay, he's just harsh because he's a perfectionist and so on. Anton was nodding and wiping away tears, his detached prop nose in his hand.

I made Hans coffee, considered what would happen if I put laxatives in it, enjoyed that thought for a good ten seconds and then headed back out through the theater, cup of boiling coffee in hand.

Soon I was behind the stage, passing by Marcus who was still warming up. He'd moved on from ominous tones to something more light-hearted. As I walked by, he switched over to Flight of the Bumblebees.

"Go quickly little bee before the 'genius' gets upset!" Marcus said in a low tone that had a smile in it.

There were a lot of people who worked with Hans and, apart from Esmeralda, who was lovely to everyone and never had a bad word to say, I was yet to meet a single one who didn't dislike Hans (or outright hate him). The lighting director, Julian, was strictly professional but whenever Hans wasn't looking, he was glaring at him. He was filling in for his brother, Andreas, who had left the production two days after they arrived in Harlot Bay. It was "stress leave" but the rumors were probably closer to the truth: Hans had abused him, and Andreas had quit because of it.

I grinned back at Marcus and then put that smile away as

5

TESS LAKE

I approached Hans' room. If I were lucky, he'd ignore me. He never said thanks for any of the coffees I'd delivered.

I knocked and waited.

He'd always say "Enter" in that tone that made people upset just hearing it.

When there was no answer, I knocked again. Should I just go in?

I heard a slight thump, like someone bumping against a desk.

Maybe he was getting changed.

I had his coffee on a small plate, and the cup rattled when my hands suddenly shook. That prickly feeling of *something is wrong* goosebumped over me.

"Mr. Holtz? I have your coffee," I called out.

Another bump from the other side of the door.

The sensation of wrongness grew stronger. That was it; I was going in.

I opened the door.

Hans had taken the largest dressing room. It had been formerly decorated with photos and posters of past productions at the Harlot Bay Playhouse. On his first day, he'd instructed me to strip them down and "take them away to be burned."

I took them away but didn't burn them. He'd then moved in an enormous desk and his furniture.

At first, I thought the room was empty, but then I saw the feet down by the side of the desk.

They were shaking.

The coffee hit the floor, and I barely felt the hot droplets that splashed back on me. I rushed across the room and found Hans flat on his back, clawing at his throat with one hand, his other flailing at the desk, hitting it.

He was foaming at the mouth, white froth with streaks of green.

He coughed and stopped breathing.

"I need help," I screamed out, hoping someone down the corridor would hear me.

I turned back to him, grabbing his feet and hauling him away from the desk to make room. I started CPR, pressing my hands over his heart.

Hans moved, hitting me with his hand. He opened it, and a piece of paper spiraled down to land on his chest. It was a note, written in scrawled letters.

The show must go on.

I kept up the CPR even as people arrived. I kept my focus on Hans until a paramedic gently pulled me aside and took over.

CHAPTER TWO

*A*fter the ambulance had taken Hans (still breathing according to the paramedics) Esmeralda dismissed us and called an end to rehearsals for the day. The teenagers immediately scattered to the four winds in an instant and then all the adults slowly followed. I walked back to my car and sat there for a moment before I decided to do what I usually do when confronted with possible murder, madness and other supernatural things: I would go to *Traveler* to see my cousins.

Molly and Luce had told me that business had been down in the last two weeks for some unknown reason. When I arrived at *Traveler*, I was expecting it to at least have a few customers, but it was empty!

Long gone were the days of double-decker tourist buses parked in the street and a line of tourists stretching out the door to get the fantastic coffee that their coffee machine, Stefano, made. Since the *Magic Bean* had opened and Tess and John Donaldson, the owners, had obtained an identical coffee machine, they had split the Harlot Bay coffee business in half. My cousins weren't exactly going to become super rich on the back of a coffee business, but they'd been doing okay, up until now.

I walked in the door, the bell above me jingling, and found my cousins *conspiring*. Conspiring was exactly the right word for it. They had a map out on the table, were circling things, had a variety of notes around them, and were hunched over like crazy, wicked witches, which I guess at the moment they pretty much *were*. Molly jumped at the sound of me entering and then quickly stuffed a piece of incriminating paper behind her back.

"What's up, family?" I said.

"You want to know what's up? I'll tell you what's up. This sandwich," Luce said. She picked up half a sandwich from a plate on the table.

"Come over here and try this," she said.

You'd think seeing a guy get poisoned, which is I guess what happened to him, and almost die, would dampen down an appetite but it was close to lunch, and my stomach growled.

So I walked over, took the sandwich from her and had a bite. It was chicken and avocado and something else delicious, some kind of sauce.

"Oh my goddess this is spectacular," I said through my mouthful of food.

"Yeah, that's a big problem for us," Molly said.

I took another bite, virtually inhaling half the sandwich before Luce snatched it out of my hands.

"Stop it. We need it for forensic analysis," Luce said.

"I want to marry that sandwich and have its children," I said, closing my eyes as I chewed.

"Oh goddess, don't say that or we're ruined," Luce moaned.

I swallowed the sandwich and opened my eyes to find that Luce had carefully moved the rest of it out of my reach.

My stomach grumbled again at being deprived of such deliciousness.

"Did you guys make that? Where did it come from?" I said.

"That sandwich came from *Magic Bean* who, by the way, *surprise*, are making sandwiches now and other delicious food," Luce said.

"That's not all. They also have a guitarist sitting in the coffee shop playing music, and he has blue eyes," Molly added in a serious tone.

"Don't forget the scruffiness. He has just the right amount of scruffiness," Luce said.

"Blue eyes and scruffiness - a deadly combination if I say so myself," I said.

"Check this out too," Luce said.

She picked up a paper bag from the table and gave it to me. On it was a logo for the *Magic Bean* that must have been new. It was beautiful and ornate, yet crisp and clear. The paper of the bag felt good as I held it in my hands.

"Can you feel the texture of that bag? These guys have stepped it up a notch," Luce said.

"Several notches. I don't think there are any more notches left. They've gotten themselves a whole new belt," Molly said. Just then Luce looked over my shoulder at someone walking by and then shouted out "Hey Kira get in here!"

I turned around to see Kira come into *Traveler* with what I think for a moment was a guilty look on her face.

"And where exactly are you going, young lady?" Luce asked, crossing her arms.

"You know where I'm going. Don't make me say it."

"But we have coffee here!"

"Do you have a scruffy blue-eyed guitarist? No."

"We could!"

"Well, when you guys get someone scruffy and handsome,

let me know, and I'll bring the kids with me. Until then, adios amigos," Kira said, turning about-face.

"Wait, aren't you two meant to be at rehearsal? What are you doing here?" Molly asked.

Kira spun around and pointed at me.

"I'm gonna let H-bomb field that one because I've got a date with a sandwich, coffee, and some dreamy blue eyes," Kira said.

"Oh twist the knife why don't you," Luce moaned again.

A moment later Kira was gone, and my cousins turned to me.

"So what happened? Someone attempt to murder Hans and rehearsal got shut down for the day?" Luce asked.

I gave a double blink.

"Yeah, that's pretty much it I think. I went to bring in his coffee, and he was foaming at the mouth and having a seizure. I think it was poison." I quickly talked them through the morning, Hans shouting and being his usual terrible self and then me discovering him in his dressing room foaming at the mouth and kicking his legs.

"Wow, that is both crazy, and I guess not unexpected," Molly said. I'd kept my cousins well informed of what it was like working for Hans over the last few weeks. They had sided with Jack in saying that no amount of money was worth the abuse that I had been experiencing. But they did sometimes see my side of things, though.

The *Harlot Bay Reader* wasn't shut down, but I'd abandoned it, the website sitting there with a thick coat of dust on it. I was down to working even fewer part-time hours at the library, only coming in on some evenings to sort papers after the library had restricted funding for that job. There had been a certain amount of money allocated to it, and Ollie had been delighted to have the opportunity to digitize so many of the old papers, many of which had been at risk of being lost forever through the natural ravages of time (and sometimes floods and mice and whatever else). But then there had been termites found in another part of the library, and unfortunately, they'd to divert some of the funding to fix that up. That had meant my job, which had already been part-time to begin with was now on even fewer hours.

You might think at this point that perhaps I could go and work for Aunt Cass, who was running the *Chili Challenge*, or perhaps the moms at the new location of *Big Pie Bakery*, but there weren't any jobs to be had there either. Aunt Cass had hired staff members to help her - three teenagers - and didn't need anyone else. The moms had the same deal. They already had staff members, and although they could throw me a shift now and then, they certainly couldn't fire somebody just to give me a job.

"I can't believe I guessed that. Do you think I could be psychic?" Luce said.

"Well, you didn't know that Jeff Larson was going to get diarrhea on that date when he took you to the ice-skating rink, so I'm going to go with *no*," Molly said. She turned back to me and gave me an appraising look.

"So what are you going to do Torrent? Get involved or stay out of it, and probably end up getting involved anyway?"

Since the Shadow Witch had come to town and stolen use of my boyfriend's body, kidnapped Kira and committed a whole bunch of other crimes and evil in pursuit of her dark plans, the three of us had had plenty of conversations about what it is we should do the next time we got pulled into some mystery. Aunt Cass had told me when I had confronted her about the various things that happen in Harlot Bay that there was something *strange* in our town.

That sounds like quite a shallow explanation considering the number of magical, mystical and murderous things that have occurred in Harlot Bay. But it was an apt description because the truth of it is, there was something strange going on, and we didn't know the source of it. Many of our conversation centered around what it was we three, as witches, were going to do about it. Privately, I had decided that I was going to investigate, that I was going to uncover, that I was going to dig and dig and dig until I got to the heart of whatever it was that was festering in Harlot Bay. I hadn't told my cousins all of this, keeping to myself that I now, like Aunt Cass, had a lair of my own. I was definitely on the side of telling the truth and being open, but at the same time, my cousins and family were very prone to freakouts, and that didn't help anyone.

"I've decided I'm going to get involved," I said moving past Molly and having a look at the table and the map they'd been drawing on.

"Are you going to need our help? The only reason I ask is that we're kind of busy with this other project," Luce said.

"Not just yet. I'll start investigating, and if something comes up, I'll be sure to get you involved. So what is this anyway?" I said, pointing at the map.

We all sat down in the booth and Molly rotated the map around, so it was the right side up for me.

"Since *Magic Bean* has stepped things up a notch, we need to step it up several notches. Refer to my previous comments regarding notches and belts if you will. They're serving delicious food, and amazing coffee and they have a live musician, so we need to do at least *that* if we're going to compete," she said.

I looked around the empty *Traveler*.

"Do you seriously think them having *amazing* food and a musician has taken all of your business away?" I asked.

"Nope, I think they're bribing bus drivers, but we don't have any proof of that. Yet!" Luce said.

Molly tapped a finger on the map.

"These are locations around Harlot Bay of closed up cafes, places that have kitchens, or the ability for us to serve food. There is a variety of them, and luckily, one is right next door. We've been trying to decide whether we should move the entire business or just expand, which seems like the easier and cheaper thing to do," Molly said.

"Oh yeah, wasn't that a diner at one point?" I said, trying to remember. Businesses were always opening and closing in Harlot Bay. It was one of the risks of a tourist town. There were often people coming from outside the community to open up a business, using their savings, thinking that they were going to retire to this lovely seaside life where they had a business for a couple of hours a day and then walked on the beach for the rest of it. The sad reality of a tourist town was that you had to try to make as much money as possible during peak tourist season, and then spend as little as possible of it during the rest of the year when you could go an entire month easily without making a single dollar.

"Yup, it was called Wilma's Diner, and it was open for just three months before it shut down," Luce said.

"Any idea what happened to Wilma?" I asked.

"Nope. But the good news is that it's been sitting there empty for so long that the Council is more than happy to let us use it under the free rent program. It has a full kitchen out the back and enough space that if we wanted we could open up a café. They've also given us permission to knock a hole through the wall and make an entrance so people can come and go to both businesses."

I looked back at the map. There was a circle around *Magic Bean*, one around *Traveler* and the empty building next to it, and a few other places that I knew were empty buildings as well, but there were some other circles drawn in red that were *definitely* not boarded-up businesses.

"Are these... witches?" I said, pointing at one of the circles.

Molly and Luce looked at each other, a quick guilty glance between them.

"We think the Donaldsons are getting help from a witch who is doing something to make the food delicious," Luce said.

"So that's a short list of possible suspects," Molly said.

"What's your plan here? You going to find some witch and say hey, are you supplying the *Magic Bean* with flavor-enhanced magic sauce?" I asked.

"We're currently still formulating the plan," Molly said. I saw Luce glance over my shoulder and widen her eyes as she looked out the front window. We both turned to see what had in the last week become a familiar sight: teenagers making out.

"Can't they find private places to kiss each other?" Molly asked.

"Yeah, just like we did, out in the woods and the forest, down dark alleyways so that no one can see you," Luce added.

"What is that boy wearing?" I mused.

The teenage boy and girl across the road were maybe fifteen or sixteen years old. The weather was getting warmer, but it wasn't *that* warm outside, certainly not enough to warrant the microscopic pair of shorts the boy was wearing. His T-shirt had been ripped with holes that looked like they had been mended with plastic tape. The girl's outfit was what we'd probably call *teenager trying too hard*. Too short in all directions.

"I know we used to wear things like that but, again, they weren't *really* like that were they?" Molly asked.

A while ago we infiltrated a teenage party in the hopes of tracking down some thieves and gotten a sudden wake-up call as to the fact that we were no longer teenagers ourselves and were slipping towards sharing the attitudes of our moms.

The couple pulled apart and then I recognized them, now that I could see their faces. The girl was Amaris, and the boy was Garrison. The both had roles in the *Taming of the Shrew.*

"Are they more Shakespeare escapees?" Luce asked.

"Yep. Out and about for the day just kissing in public."

"They both need to get hold of themselves. It's not proper," Molly said, sounding like an eighty-year-old dowager.

Apparently, Molly forgot what "proper" meant a moment later when the door jangled and Ollie came walking in. He spent a lot of time at the library and often had a vest or waistcoat and shirt combination going on. Today, perhaps in deference to the warmer weather, he'd done away with the vest and was just wearing a white shirt with the top button undone. Molly flung herself at him and practically smooched the poor boy into the ground. When they pulled apart his cheeks were going red, his hair was messed up, and his eyes were starting to go wild. He turned towards us and awkwardly smiled before clearing his throat.

"Hey, everyone, good to see you," he said.

"No, it's *so* good to see you," Molly cooed, still holding his arm and then leaning forward giving him kisses on the neck.

"Um, Harlow, I had some papers that I found, that research you asked me to do. I figured you might come by here for lunch," Ollie said. He came over to the table, practically dragging Molly along with him and handed me a sheaf of photocopied documents. I looked through them, seeing they were are a mix of newspaper articles and lists of names.

Not too long ago I'd had somewhat of a breakthrough with John Smith, the ghost who I'd been working with for years to help him move on. John had a severe memory problem. He didn't remember a wife or children, where he lived, how old he had been, any jobs he had done. He occasionally displayed knowledge that he had lived in the town for quite a while, but it was never enough to tie him to any historical period with any accuracy. Quite a long time ago he'd called me *Talica Moore*, a person it seemed he was very fond of, before forgetting who she was. That name had led nowhere. Through all of my searching, I'd never discovered a connection to anything to do with Harlot Bay. Then one random afternoon I had awoken to John looming over me in my office, and I blurted out to him *who was Talica Moore?* Suddenly, John had changed, growing younger until he was about in his early thirties and wearing a straw boater hat and striped clothing that very strongly suggested he was a singer in an acapella group. With this one clue, I'd put Harlot Bay's lead researcher on the case and asked Ollie to find me every single acapella group that ever existed in Harlot Bay and surrounding areas to see if we could track down who John might be. I briefly flicked through the papers, seeing that some of the articles even had photographs with them, albeit in black and white and not very clear.

"I came across a bunch of church newsletters that happened to list different music groups who were playing for them, and then that made it a lot easier to track down their names and the people who were singing in them. There's no one called John Smith, but it's possible that whoever you're looking for might be under another name," Ollie said.

"You are *so* wonderful, Ollie. Thank you so much for helping Harlow," Molly said. Then she looked at me and raised her eyebrows. "I trust that's enough research for you to get on with? That you won't need Ollie to do anything else for you?" she asked. The pointed tone might have gone straight over Ollie's head, but to me, it was crystal clear. What she was saying was "Don't get my boyfriend involved."

Jack was the only one of our three boyfriends who knew

that we were witches. Ollie and Will were still unaware. I had asked Ollie to investigate the name John Smith and all the acapella groups, and told him it was for an article for the *Harlot Bay Reader*. Despite the fact that the Reader was collapsing down to nothing and he knew I was barely working on it, he'd still helped me because he's just that kind of guy, and also, he *loves* to do research.

"Yes, that might be good for now," I said, somewhat noncommittally. I didn't want to tell Molly at that moment that I had in fact given Ollie quite a few research jobs to do, dealing with digging into the deep past of Harlot Bay. I also had him looking into the past of my family, trying to put together a family tree and also one for Juliet Stern, who was somehow related to Hattie Stern. That request I'd covered with a small lie saying that some of us in our family were interested to know our family tree. As before, Ollie had agreed to help without asking any further questions.

"Right, well, I need to go to work now," Ollie said. He glanced down at the map covered in circles, and then at my two cousins. His eyes narrowed slightly.

"Are the three of you planning something again? Because this right here looks suspicious," he said.

"Nope, just looking for locations to expand our café," Luce said, grabbing the map, all the bits of paper, and folding them all up at once, looking in fact super guilty and that we were *definitely* planning something.

Molly gave Ollie another passionate kiss, and then he finally extricated himself from her arms and left, the door jingling behind him. Molly turned on me the moment he was gone. "I don't want you to give him any more jobs to look into anything. I don't want him involved!" she said, pointing a finger at me.

"But he's the best researcher in Harlot Bay. He loves it,

and let's face the truth, we need all the help that we can get," I said.

"I want to tell him that I'm a witch when *I'm* ready to tell him that I'm a witch. I don't want him to come across some weird ghost thing in all the papers and then it's a surprise," Molly said.

"It was a surprise for Jack, and he took it fine," I said, somewhat snarkily, crossing my arms.

"Maybe we should work out when we're going to tell them," Luce said. Molly started to speak, the morning threatening to careen off into an argument when the door jangled again and in came Peta.

"Harlow? What happened? The theater is closed and there was no one there."

I jumped out of my seat.

"Oh my goddess, I'm sorry, you were out with Henry G weren't you? We think Hans got poisoned," I said in a rush.

Peta had returned to town around Christmas and had thus far been a little like me, somewhat adrift, sliding towards poverty, and trying to work out what job she could do or even if they were jobs available in Harlot Bay for her. She'd been an architect in a past life, and then it slipped sideways into doing interior design but had finally decided it wasn't the life for her and so had returned to Harlot Bay. She was dating Jack's half-brother Jonas, and when I had gotten a job working on the theater production so had she, as assistant to the costumer Henry G.

Peta sat down with us, and I quickly went back through the story of what had happened in the morning. Luce didn't notice that Peta picked up the sandwich from the *Magic Bean* and had taken a bite while I was telling the story.

"Wow, that's terrible, but I can't help but feel like the guy deserved it," Peta said.

"That's what I said!" Molly said.

"I know this is a terrible story but can I just say this sandwich is amazing. Did you guys make this?" Peta said

She popped the last of it into her mouth.

"No, we needed that for forensic analysis!" Luce wailed.

"Sorry. It was just too good," Peta said.

"So anyway, rehearsals are shut down for today but I think we're going back tomorrow," I finished.

"Do you think Hans is going to be okay?" Peta asked.

"The paramedic said he was still breathing when they took him but, honestly it didn't look good. I think green foam coming out of your mouth isn't a great sign," I said.

Now, it might sound as though the four of us are quite callous and uncaring people who were very unconcerned that Hans had been poisoned and might be dead. But he was the most horrendous man I'd ever met, I think, short of Sylvester Coldwell, the slippery real estate agent who was involved in various crimes around Harlot Bay. I have rarely hated anyone, but it was easy to say that I hated Hans. He was arrogant and cruel, yelling at teenagers, demanding coffees, being abrupt and merciless. I don't think he enjoyed his life unless he made someone cry every single day. So you shouldn't judge us too harshly when Peta clapped her hands and said "Next topic, I don't care," out loud and the four of us started talking about her and Jonas, and then Molly and Luce's plans to open a café next door, the rash of teenagers around town making out everywhere, and then finally plans for what we might do on the weekend. We might have sat there for hours just chatting but finally, a small tourist bus parked out the front and a group of customers came in, looking around the empty *Traveler* as though they were unsure whether it was safe to enter.

"Okay, well I've got pick up some more fabrics for Henry G, so I'll see you all later," Peta said.

We all said goodbye, me leaving my cousins behind to

begin serving coffee. I went back to my car, and started up the engine to drive up the hill and back home. Despite the fact, I had seen Hans frothing green at the mouth, and I had to give him CPR in an attempt to save his life, that moment quickly slipped out of my mind. I admit it was a little bit odd because typically such horrific things stick with you, but the truth of it was I had much bigger fish to fry. Perhaps whales to fry or some other gigantic sea creature like maybe a Kraken. With an unexpected afternoon off, the moms busy at the bakery, Aunt Cass likely at the *Chili Challenge*, and my cousins away, I decided to take myself off to my secret lair.

CHAPTER THREE

I was in my lair staring at my wall of crazy when Adams stepped out of the shadows and dropped a cat bowtie at my feet.

"Good, you're here, put that on me," he said.

"Put that on me *please*," I replied.

Adams frowned.

"Why are you saying please to me? Put my bowtie on me now," he demanded.

I held my tongue but rolled my eyes. Cats were very much like toddlers, quite abrupt and with little knowledge of social niceties. In fact, they were probably worse than toddlers because least a toddler wouldn't scratch you if you didn't do what it wanted. I crouched down and clipped the small cat bowtie around his neck and then straightened it up.

"So why do you want a bowtie, Mr. Fancy Cat?" I asked.

"It's private," Adams said. He stepped past me, heading for another shadow against the wall.

But I was suddenly curious.

"No, tell me, why do you need a bowtie?" I said. Adams bolted around the corner of an old desk, and I took two steps before stopping myself. There was no point chasing him. He was already gone, disappearing into the darkness the way only a magic cat can. As much as I was intensely curious about why Adams would want to wear a cat bowtie and even thought for a moment that I should come marching out of the cottage where I had set up my lair to see whether I could find him, I fought off these urges and turned my gaze back to the *wall of crazy*. Right in the center of it were two cards where I'd written in big bold letters *You have a spell cast upon you*. On the next one, it said *The spell tries to stop you knowing anything about itself. So don't get distracted!*

There were other bits of paper and things stuck to the wall, including a map of Harlot Bay where I had started making notations indicating where strange things had occurred or murders had taken place. If anyone were to see this, I'm sure they would think I was crazy which is why I thought of it as my *crazy* wall. I had marked on it where Preston Jacobs, working with or under the control of a supernatural entity, had killed a competitor for the Butter Festival. I had the locations where a little girl Holly and her dad were murdered; places where fires had taken place; sabotage on a movie set; thefts under the control of an entity named Slink that my mother had locked away; and finally the Shadow Witch, the evil witch from the deep past who had attempted to steal Kira Stern's body using most of my life force to do it.

I'd even been back through some of the histories of Harlot Bay and marked up other things on the map. The one location that was missing was the creepy mansion that was out on Truer Island.

Molly, Luce and I had found a map in a hidden room under the Torrent mansion. The room had had a spell upon it - when we had walked in, it appeared new, but the moment we had touched anything, it had transformed to old as though centuries of aging had caught up with it in an instant. There had been a diary in the room which had turned to dust, but there had also been a map which had survived. It had led us out to an empty field on Truer Island where hidden behind an enormously powerful concealment spell, there was a mansion that looked very similar to our Torrent mansion. We'd gone inside to discover a backpack full of food and wine sitting by a dinner table set out for three. We'd been shuffling our way deeper into the mansion, heading for some stairs that led downwards, when I had glanced at my cousins and saw red crowns of light around their heads, indicating that they, and me, were under the influence of a spell. I pulled us out of there, and we had only barely escaped. The moment we were away from the creepy mansion we were free of the spell, and so we had bolted. We quickly discovered after that that we could not find our way back to the mansion, that it had become hidden from us once more.

All I had up on the wall was a note: there is a creepy magical house on Truer Island.

Looking at the crazy wall was certainly an exercise in trying not to go mad. I had bought color-coded wool and tried to set up a categorization system. Things marked in red meant it was supernatural; things in black meant someone had died; things in yellow meant the Stern witches were involved, yellow being the color of lemons they grew out on their farm. But my system was struggling under the weight of everything that I'd put up on the wall. There had been murders, arson, thefts, and these were just the things that the Torrent witches had been *directly* involved in. Aunt Cass had fought some strange monster out on Truer Island, and when she defeated it, there had been an explosion so large it had detonated a gigantically deep hole about half a mile across which the authorities, unaware that magic had been involved, had blamed on a hidden gas pocket exploding.

I had even marked up on the wall where and when I'd slipped and then what had happened to me, as far as I could remember.

When I had decided a while ago that I would need a lair just like Aunt Cass so I could sit and investigate, I hadn't imagined that I would find one so easily and then that it would become a place I was both strangely attracted to and oddly repelled from. Up behind the Torrent mansion generations of Torrents had built things and then abandoned them. There were countless wells around the place, some of them full to the brim and croaking with frogs, and others bone dry. Some of them Aunt Cass and I used to help reduce the chance that we might slip, going out to boil water (after getting all the frogs out of course) and trying to float rocks around and things like that. There were numerous cottages built around the place, some of them little more than a square of stones, an outline of a building that once stood, others in ruinous states of decay with collapsed walls, and some still standing and whole.

It was in one of these that I had set up my lair, finding a cottage that was still in somewhat good condition. It was built of stones bonded together with a thick mortar and inside had a wood fire stove, a long wooden bench, and a small window on each side of the cottage. It was surprisingly well insulated but if I wanted to be in there when it was cold all I had to do was throw a chunk of wood into the stove and start it burning and the cottage would heat up quickly. Because it was largely empty I was able to fill the entire wall with the great mess of crazy. I had expanded onto the other wall with notes about John Smith, Talica Moore, his acapella costume, and anything else I could remember, such as the fact I'd seen John wearing a red crown of light as well that had streaked down to a wound on his chest.

I took my gaze off the wall and walked over to the small

desk and chair that I had hauled out there and sat down. I tried to make myself focus on the research that Ollie had provided me, but I was failing badly. Part of me knew it was simply the dry nature of the research, the list of names of people from the past, but there was another part of me deeper down that suspected it was the spell pushing against me.

A while ago I'd gone to see Hattie Stern, who I'd discovered had been carrying a note around in her pocket that had written on it: *Harlow Torrent has a spell cast upon her. Help her.* Hattie had made me promise that I would visit her so we could work on this problem and I had indeed promised her but then... I had broken that promise. It's not that I hadn't tried. The first time I attempted to go out there, although I felt embarrassed and stupid as though she didn't want me there, I had managed to get halfway to her house before my car broke down. That little ordeal had cost me a chunk of money out of my bank account that I couldn't afford and by the time it was resolved, I'd forgotten that I'd even been going to Hattie's in the first place. The next time I had remembered that I was going to go out there the front door to the mansion had become inexplicably stuck and when I heaved on it I ripped the doorknob out of the door. That had necessitated more spending of money to buy a new door, but thankfully it hadn't been so bad because Jack, my handyman boyfriend, had come round to install it for us. Since then it had crossed my mind a few times that I should visit Hattie but it was only ever a fleeting thought.

I forced myself to look back at the wall. I had a single note card up there that said *Juliet Stern's journal*. Hattie had given it to me and at first glance, it appeared to be a mundane journal of the workings of the Merchant Arms. Most of the entries were about the number of eggs she bought and pounds of flour and ingredients for making beer but hidden amongst them, and sometimes appearing and disappearing, were notes Juliet made about working with an unnamed Torrent witch, going on the *hunt*.

I had discovered that Juliet and this unnamed Torrent witch had been hunting the Shadow Witch, an evil witch who had found a type of immortality. She would use her power to push a witch out of her body and then steal it for her own, living for hundreds of years, repeating the process over the centuries. It appeared that Juliet had imbued her journal with magic, and when I'd been reading an entry I'd been pulled into a vision of the past, riding along inside my ancestor's head and experiencing her memory. I had seen the horrific past. The Torrent witch's daughter, Rosetta and Juliet's daughter, Zelda, had been trapped by the Shadow Witch.

The Shadow Witch had almost killed Rosetta, pulling her life force out and using it to propel Zelda's spirit out of her body before stealing it and escaping. Rosetta had survived and when my ancestor had been looking at Juliet, she had seen her aura, which had been golden, begin to streak with black as Juliet grieved for her dead daughter.

It had only been a vision of the past but when I'd returned to the present the journal held a weapon - a locket imbued with power that Juliet and the Torrent witch had left to be found to fight the Shadow Witch when she reappeared. It had been the only thing that had saved me, Kira and Jack and had helped destroy the Shadow Witch.

Since then I'd spent time reading the diary hoping that more could be found in it, but it had seemingly returned to its mundane state, being lists of eggs and pounds of flour. I'd given Aunt Cass and the moms a description of what had happened to me, what I'd seen in the past, and although on the day when I had told them it felt like the most important thing that had ever happened to us and that we must immediately look into it and discover everything we could, very quickly afterwards we returned to normality, the moms focused on their bakery, Aunt Cass on the *Chili Challenge*, my cousins on their business, and me back on my life. Again, in some moments I realized that this was normal, that you could not be in such a heightened state always, but in others, I realized it was the spell again seeking to hide by making us *forget*.

"Come on Harlow, pay attention now," I said to myself, standing up and pacing around. But it was no use. I looked at the great mess on the wall, following strings and strands, not seeming to be able to unravel it. I saw my notes about John Smith's wound, his comments about the past, but I could still not see any gaps and holes I could focus on to solve this.

Eventually I sat down at the desk, opened my laptop and read through a story I'd been writing. I don't quite know *how* I'd slipped into it… it felt like another kind of spell honestly. Being I was a journalist I enjoyed writing but now my journalism business was shut down and I was trying to work out what I could do with my life. At some point in between *not* looking at the wall and *not* figuring out the past, I had opened up a new file on my computer and started telling the story of a girl who was a ghost trapped in a town with very little memory of the past, and who was stuck that way until one day a man came near her and she turned solid and real, able to reconnect with the world but only when he was close.

I read over my story for a little while then switched off that and started thinking about Hans again. I hit the internet to look up all of his past misdeeds. It was quite surprising with the spotty telecommunications over Harlot Bay and how far I was from the house but the internet still worked. I'd done some vague research on Hans before I'd gone to work for him, finding that he had been stabbed in the past and been involved in plenty of other terrible events mostly caused by him. This time I came across his autobiography. It was called *'I am Shakespeare's Son - The Madness of Shakespearean Life'*. I looked through the reviews online and saw there were many praising the raw and gritty open nature of the book but just as many calling Hans an arrogant stuck up buffoon who believed he was the second coming of Shakespeare himself, and various things like that. I was just wondering whether I should order it online or whether the Book Bank in town would have it, when I saw movement out of the corner of my eye.

It was Aunt Cass and, well, she was *sneaking*. There was no other word for it. She was sneaking up to one of the other cottages. She opened the door and went inside while I sat at my desk as still as could be, carefully watching. Unlike Aunt Cass's underground lair I hadn't cast a spell on mine to keep people away from it. I had tried for a little while but the way spells work is that if you keep them going, every day at the time you cast it, it will drain your energy again. It was incredibly dangerous to keep spells going for a long time if you weren't strong enough. So I'd cast my spell at three in the afternoon and then the next day had yawned when a wave of tiredness came over me again. The next day, I'd almost fallen asleep and on the fourth day I let the spell go lest it knock me out entirely. Witches have died trying to keep too many spells going. It was yet again another reminder of how powerful Aunt Cass was given that she permanently seemed to have a spell set up to keep us away from her underground lair, and seemed quite spritely for someone who was in her eighties.

It wasn't long before Aunt Cass emerged from the cottage and my curiosity shot through the roof. She was now wearing coveralls looking like a plumber of some type and over her shoulder she had a bundle of ropes and what appeared to be rock climbing gear. She was wearing a belt that looked like you could connect ropes to it if you were going to scale a mountain. She closed the cottage behind her and then walked off down the hill. I sat there for all of a minute having an internal battle with myself about whether I should follow her. I finally decided I should because if I caught her wearing coveralls and carrying ropes, there's no way she would be able to deny that she wasn't up to something.

I quickly shut my laptop and crept out of the cottage, promising myself I'd come back later to retrieve it before I headed down the hill. When Aunt Cass disappeared around the front of the mansion I increased my speed, jogging after her, afraid she was going to pull an Adams on me. When I came around the corner, my heart sank when it appeared that she had. Aunt Cass was nowhere to be seen. My moment of disappointment didn't last long, though, because I heard the familiar sound of Jack's truck and then he was pulling up outside the mansion. He came bounding out of the truck and raced over to me before grabbing me in his arms and pulling me against him.

"Are you okay? I just talked to Jonas. He said that Hans guy got poisoned and you saw it?" he said.

"I'm not upset about it," I said somewhat muffled from somewhere in the vicinity of his chest. Jack let me go and looked at me. As I said before, the combination of scruffiness and blue eyes is quite deadly.

Jack's eyes hovered on a point somewhere between blue and green and seemed to shift with the light. At the moment, in the shade of the Torrent mansion, they were a deeper blue as though if I peered into them I would be looking into the ocean and somewhere in the cool water I would find colorful coral. Jack pointed his finger at me.

"Do not tell the police that you weren't upset about the guy getting poisoned. Everyone knows who he is. Everyone knows he was hated, but police love nothing more than finding people who hated a victim and trying to pin it on them," Jack said.

"I'll tell the police it was very distressing if they come to ask me," I said.

Jack paused for a moment and then pointed back at his truck.

"I know I've never done this before, but I made you cookies," he said. He grabbed me by the hand and pulled me back to his truck where he had, in fact, a container of choc chip cookies, still warm from the oven. He told me he'd finished work early and for some reason felt like making them, only discovering as they were coming out of the oven when he was talking to Jonas what had happened today. We went inside and started eating cookies which led us somewhat to ruining dinner, but it didn't matter at all.

Molly and Luce came home and brought their boyfriends Will and Ollie, and a whole bunch of takeaway Indian. The six of us ate delicious Indian, and then we opened a couple of bottles of wine and drank them and demolished the rest of Jack's choc chip cookies before the night drew to a close.

It wasn't long before Jack and I were in the warm dark of my bedroom. I leaned forward and kissed him and then whispered in his ear "Thank you for the cookies."

CHAPTER FOUR

I was at rehearsals talking with Henry G, the chief costumer, and Peta when I Slipped. Sometimes in the past when I'd slipped I'd have no idea until something weird started happening like the ground turning soupy or flowers starting to grow spikes.

This was *not* one of those times. I was standing chatting to Henry G about the fabulous costume that he had constructed for Katherine, played by Kira, when I heard what sounded like a distant explosion. The magic surged and cold bubbles rushed up my legs as though I'd plunged into an icy swimming pool. They fizzed up my body and out the top of my head, leaving a trail of goosebumps behind them. I gasped, and flinched involuntarily.

"Are you okay darling?" Henry G said and raised one of his finally sculpted eyebrows.

"Yeah, just a random shiver," I said, slipping back to the lie I'd used many times in the past to explain why I might suddenly jerk and then be looking around as though I was stunned.

"Oh no, you're not getting sick, are you?" Henry G said

and touched me on the back of the hand. I heard a croak of a frog next to my ear, incredibly loud and then an echoing chorus of them fading away. Somewhere behind it I heard someone shouting:

"Notable coward, an infinite and endless liar, an hourly promise breaker, the owner of no one good quality!"

Behind that, which I recognized as an insult from one of Shakespeare's plays, there was the another voice shouting "Away you 3-inch fool, I am sick when I do look on thee."

They echoed away, leaving me blinking at Henry G who was watching me with a half smile on his lips and Peta who wore a mask of concern. She knew exactly what was going on. She'd been my friend my entire life and had known that I was a Slip witch for just as long.

"Darling, you can't jump like that around a man who carries so many pins in his hands," Henry G quipped and patted me on the hand again.

"Maybe you shivered because you remembered seeing Hans get poisoned yesterday," Peta said, obviously ad-libbing to move the focus off me.

"Oh, I do not care at all that that horrible man got poisoned," Henry G said.

Peta smiled and smacked him on the back of the hand.

"Don't let the police hear you say that or you're going be going to jail," she said.

"I don't mind an interview with the police, it could be quite fun. I hear there are some quite handsome policemen in this town," Henry G said. I laughed, despite what I was feeling, terribly afraid that a costume would burst into flames or something else odd would happen. I quickly excused myself and went to the kitchen where I grabbed a glass of water and stood there at the sink while I drank it, feeling the cool liquid plume down into my stomach.

"Please, nothing serious, please, nothing serious," I

murmured to myself, the endless prayer of a Slip witch. There were so many things that being a Slip witch had ruined in my life. There were teenage parties that I'd missed because I'd slipped, and couldn't attend without being a danger. I had almost missed my graduation when I had slipped and people started hearing a high-pitched whining in their ears whenever I was near them. Aunt Cass had quickly whipped up a potion and dosed me with it. It had left me feeling somewhat ill, but at least I had been able to attend my graduation for a few hours before it wore off. I'd had to leave because people thought there was something wrong with the speaker system. They were just *mild* examples of how bad being a Slip witch could be. When I was a child I had slipped and if I came too near a tree it would explode into splinters. I'd been forced to stay in the house for a week, my mother telling the school that I'd come down with a particularly nasty flu.

I quickly rinsed my glass and then walked back out and around behind the stage. Esmeralda had gathered us all to rehearse and then told us that a new director would be coming today but that we'd have to wait to meet him. In the meantime, we'd rehearse the play until he arrived. Unfortunately, that meant a lot of sitting around for certain characters and when teenagers sat around and got bored, they got into mischief. Part of my job, apart from being a general assistant, was starting to feel like being a teenage wrangler. I would have to retrieve them from whatever dark corner they'd crept off to and unfortunately I'd come upon a few too many teenagers with askew clothing and red faces. Again, I remembered what it was like to be a teenager and all the things Molly, Luce and I had done, but at the same time it felt like we'd *never* been like this. I was wandering around when Esmeralda touched me on the arm to speak with me.

I heard a sudden burst of applause as though I was

surrounded by a crowd who were jubilant about something. There was cheering and whistling and then wine glasses clinking together before finally, the noise of a door closing. It all came and went in a moment.

"May you please find Amaris for me, we're about to rehearse the auction," Esmeralda said and gave me a warm smile.

"Sure I'll get her," I said my mind reeling. Okay, that was two lots of sounds when people had touched me in the last few minutes. First it had been frogs and Shakespearean insults when Henry G touched me, and now applause and wine glasses when it was Esmeralda. So was I hearing sounds connected to who they were or what they did? It wasn't too hard to put it together. Shakespearean insults and shouting could easily be linked to Henry G and Hans. Henry G had worked for Hans for just a year but had also privately told us that he did not like the man at all but considered that working with him was a good career move for any costumer. Esmeralda's sounds were applause and wine glasses, which made sense too. The applause because she worked in theater, and the wine glasses because she was frequently attending benefits to raise money for other theater productions across the country. I was a little puzzled as to why I would hear frogs when Henry G touched me but perhaps he owned a frog? Or who knew, it might just be some weird quirk of the Slip witch power.

As I walked off to find Amaris I passed by a teenage boy. I didn't know his name given there were quite a few of them working on the play, but I lightly touched him on the shoulder as I went by to see if I could trigger the Slip witch power again. Nothing happened, however. He just glanced at me and moved to the side as I passed.

Damn, I thought I'd figured it out.

I walked around out into the theater and down into the

rooms that stretched out behind it. Like many of the old buildings in Harlot Bay, this one had plenty of rooms leading off each other and then also little secret areas. There was a trapdoor in one of the rooms that was permanently bolted shut that led to another floor beneath the theater. I had no doubt there were probably other hidden areas as well, left over from when pirates used to roam up and down the coast and come raiding, or for when prohibition was in effect and it seemed the whole of Harlot Bay had been secretly making and hiding alcohol.

I wasn't creeping exactly and I certainly didn't have any intention to catch teenagers doing something they shouldn't, but I must've been thinking and not realizing that I was sneaking in the process. I heard Amaris speak from the other side of an open door.

"You want to date me? Then prove your love for me," she said.

Amaris was playing Bianca, the younger daughter who could not marry until her older sister Katherine, the "shrew", was married. For a moment I thought Amaris was rehearsing, perhaps saying a line from the play but then I glanced into the room and saw she was standing there with three of the boys in front of her. Their names were Fox, Cormac, and Stone. I wasn't entirely sure which one was Cormac and which one was Stone because they looked quite similar, and I hadn't quite got a grip on all the teenagers' names.

"How do we prove our love?" Fox asked.

"Steal something for me," Amaris said. She turned and with a perfect hair flip flounced out of there, the three boys watching her go, desperate looks on their faces.

I shrank back into a hiding place and a moment later Amaris walked by me, heading back to the main part of the stage. I didn't hear the boys talk but it wasn't long before they came wandering out as well. One of them, I'm not sure if it was Stone or Cormac, had red eyes like he'd been crying.

"I'm the one she loves," he muttered to himself as he went by, low enough that the other two boys didn't hear.

I waited a good thirty seconds, shaking my head to myself at what I'd just seen. Apart from wrangling teenagers, I'd also been wrangling teenage drama. It seemed that all of their emotions were turned up to ten or twenty, or possibly a million. Small failures were tragedies, small successes were awesome and amazing and the best thing ever! They were so happy when they got their lines right and so devastated when they got it wrong. I wasn't keeping a careful track of which relationships were going on, but I'm pretty sure that there had already been at least five or six break ups and new couples formed over the course of the rehearsal. But this? Amaris telling them to steal something to prove their love for her? This was new. I felt like I was watching the news and they say something crazy like "Teenagers robbing stores to prove their love. We reveal the shocking story" and it's so far outside of your comprehension you just don't know what to think. It sounds true but at the same time, it sounds *crazy*.

I remembered a time when Molly and I had crept around following a boy that Molly had been interested in, effectively stalking him around the town for a couple of hours and even using concealment spells so he wouldn't see us.

Yeah, teenagers can be crazy.

I made my way back to the main part of the stage and found Amaris who was now talking with Vienna. I told her to get ready to rehearse her scene, deciding I would think a little more on what I had witnessed before I would take any action, if at all. I know to the teenagers their dramas seemed real and vibrant and important, but I could also feel some distance from them and a little bit of me didn't want to get involved that much. I certainly had enough on my plate as it was. I didn't want any of the boys to get arrested for stealing stuff though, at least even from the position that it would make putting on the play quite difficult.

Esmeralda called all the actors in and was getting ready to run the scene when the doors to the theater boomed open. In strolled a well-dressed round man with slicked back hair and a beaming smile. Everyone stopped to watch him as he walked down the aisle, looking around him, as though he couldn't be happier to be here.

"My name is Emilion Rain. That is a mouthful so just call me director!" He waved his arms as he spoke as if punctuating his sentences with his hands.

"Oh look at all you beautiful people. Have I walked into a theater of actors or fish who stare with their mouths open?" he boomed. If Hans had said such a thing, it would have easily been a grievous insult, born from a place of meanness but Emilion, or the Director as he told us to call him, was beaming, glowing with an inner joy that you could feel. I had a sudden feeling in my stomach of relaxation and happiness and realized that I had been a bit tense since I discovered a new director would be coming. Perhaps I'd been traumatized so much by Hans and his abuse that I expected all directors to be like that.

He came and embraced Esmeralda, kissing her on both cheeks, before taking a copy of the play and calling the teenagers to "Begin! Begin my darlings!" He stood and watched as the teenagers hesitantly began the scene. They were only a few lines into it before he waved his arms for them to stop.

"I know you're all terribly shocked that the previous director has suffered great ill, but don't worry. Together we will get to the end and we will succeed. Now go again with passion, with love, with joy, you can do it. I believe in you," he said. The teenagers began again and this time it seemed as though the director had infused them with great confidence. I swear some of them became better actors on the spot, delivering their lines the way they were meant to be. As Molly would say, stepping it up several notches to the point of needing a new belt.

The rehearsal was underway and we smoothly went through that scene and then to another, jumping around the play. Normally when Hans was in charge people would attempt to disappear if they weren't in a particular scene, so that he couldn't turn his wrath upon them. But everything was completely different now with Emilion in charge. Practically everyone was gathered around watching the scenes, seeing just how wonderful it could be when everything came together. One of the girls, Frankie, who had been dropping lines all over the place was delivering them with confidence, as though that inner glow had transferred from the director to her.

Time quickly zipped by. I met Emilion briefly and when he shook my hand I didn't hear anything. There was no magic burst.

We'd been rehearsing for a few hours, the director changing some of the blocking, which was the movements around on stage when Sheriff Hardy and some of his men entered the theater. We'd been told that the police would be becoming today to do some brief interviews about Hans. Sheriff Hardy caught my eye and nodded. Although he was now official and on-the-job and had to interview me as part of that, the nod also carried a familiarity, being that he was dating Aunt Ro and in fact would be coming to the big family dinner tonight.

"Who is *that* handsome man?" Henry G murmured to me as Sheriff Hardy walked down the aisle.

"That is Sheriff Hardy and he's dating my aunt so sorry, he's taken," I said.

"Oh well, there's plenty more fish in the sea," he said.

Everyone milled around as Sheriff Hardy talked with Emilion. I had no sudden intuition that something was about to go terribly wrong. There was no Slip witch power that told it to me, but I must've heard something, perhaps a creaking because I felt a sudden burst of anxiety.

A bare moment later there was a snap from high above us.

Christopher, the teenager who was coincidentally playing Christopher Sly, the drunken Tinker who is duped into believing he is a Lord, went from standing to flat on the ground, out cold, a heavy sandbag thudding him down. One of the girls screamed a piercing sound that echoed across the theater.

"EVERYONE OFF THE STAGE!" Sheriff Hardy yelled out. We all scattered, teenagers leaping off the stage and not a moment too soon. There was another creak and a heavy sandbag thudded to the stage. I grabbed Christopher's arm and with Sheriff Hardy's help, hauled him off the stage. There was one final creak from above and then another thud as a heavy sandbag dropped and crashed on the boards.

"Everyone outside now. No one goes anywhere," Sheriff Hardy said. He checked Christopher, who was stirring. It looked like the bag had only caught him a glancing blow, knocking him out rather than seriously injuring him.

The teenagers certainly didn't have to be told twice, the mass of them rushing up to the front door, everyone talking all at once.

I'd only ever seen Esmeralda happy, even through Hans yelling, even through teenage drama, forgetting their lines and rushing off the stage in tears, and so it was a shock to see her start crying.

"We're cursed. We need to shut down," she moaned from behind her hands.

Sheriff Hardy looked at her and then at me.

"You're not cursed, someone's doing this deliberately," he said. "We're going to find out who it is and stop them," he said.

Some of his men helped an unsteady Christopher outside, so they could wait for an ambulance to take him to the hospital to get him checked out. It felt for an odd moment that when Sheriff Hardy said "We're going to stop them" that he included *me* in that. I followed the Emilion outside but before the doors closed I heard another sandbag thunk to the stage.

"The show must go on," Emilion said to me and then raised his voice so the assembled teenagers and actors could hear.

"The show must go on. Now let us continue to rehearse," he said. Despite the terror of the moment, most of the teenagers began smiling back at him. There was a kind of energy as though something horrific had occurred but now if we banded together we could all get through it.

Christopher clearly didn't feel the same.

"No, I'm out, I'm done. I'm not gonna be in this stupid thing where people keep dying," he said. He staggered off down the street, closely followed by a police officer who was trying to convince him to stay put.

"We'll find someone to replace him," Emilion said. As I watched Christopher staggering off down the street, the police officer close behind, I couldn't help but feel that all of us should do the same. Someone had poisoned Hans and now it appeared they had sabotaged heavy sandbags in the hope of injuring others. Perhaps Esmeralda was right: maybe the play was cursed.

CHAPTER FIVE

"So no one else got told to invite someone crazy?" Peta asked us. Everyone shook their heads.

"Aunt Cass is definitely up to something," Luce said.

The eight of us were gathered in our end of Torrent mansion for a pre-dinner planning session for if and when the whole thing went off the rails. It was me, Molly and Luce, our respective three boyfriends Jack, Will and Ollie, and also Peta and Jonas. We'd just been discussing safe topics we could go onto in case things went a little crazy when Peta had revealed that Aunt Cass had told her to invite someone crazy, and then Ollie and Will had revealed they'd been told the same.

"Did you invite anyone crazy?" I asked Ollie and Will.

"I was gonna bring my dad but, then I figured maybe Cass was just being… you know," Will said.

"Same for me. I decided not to bring anyone," Ollie said.

I noticed they both had carefully skipped around outright calling Aunt Cass *crazy*. At our huge Christmas dinner there had been a magical mishap that had ultimately resulted in Aunt

Cass bolting out into the snow and disappearing around the corner of the mansion up into the forest. Given that we hadn't told Will and Ollie that we were witches and that magical mishaps were something that quite frequently happened to our family, we had to explain it away by saying that Aunt Cass was a little bit crazy, or letting Will and Ollie assume she was. It wasn't entirely off the mark. After all, they had clear memories of another dinner where Aunt Cass had brought out the *Chili Challenge*, which had resulted in our guest that night, Bella Bing, Aunt Cass and Molly all passing out after eating a super spicy chili sauce. Both the boys had been at other dinners that had gone off the rails in various other ways.

"Did you invite someone crazy?" Jonas asked Peta.

"Well, sorta. I mean he's not crazy. It's just Henry G, from the play, the costume designer. He's not crazy, he's just... effervescent."

"Effervescent, I love it," Molly trilled. She was smiling too much for someone who was facing down a Torrent witches dinner.

"You seem awfully happy," Luce said.

"Stop worrying everyone. It'll be fine. Just drink some wine," Molly rhymed.

"Now I think *you're* up to something as well as Aunt Cass," Luce said.

Our pre-dinner planning had been going reasonably well until we'd also discovered that it had been Aunt Cass who'd been the one to set up this dinner. Well *set up* is a relative term. Perhaps it would be more accurate to say that she demanded the dinner and then the moms had been put into service to make it happen. We'd only discovered this because Aunt Freya had complained to Luce about how much cooking they'd to do at short notice.

"Is your aunt okay?" Ollie asked, a little hesitantly.

"She's just Aunt Cass being Aunt Cass again and again," I said.

We all knew there was some big announcement tonight but no one had any idea of what it might be. As far as we knew the bakery was going okay and so was Aunt Cass's *Chili Challenge*. My cousins still didn't have many customers but they had a plan in motion, and I certainly didn't have any big news. So we weren't quite sure what it was going to be.

"I wonder why she would want us to invite crazy people?" Will mused.

I and Luce shared a look. Molly didn't take part because she was still too happy about whatever it was. Our look said, "Uh oh, better move on because we can't discuss the fact that we're witches and something crazy is probably going on."

"What we need is a code word for when things go totally off the rails. You can just say it and we'll change the topic or escape to retrieve another bottle of wine or something like that," Luce said.

"What was that code word we had when we were teenagers?" Peta asked.

"Chika cha!" Molly said. She was practically dancing around now, humming to herself.

"Chika cha? Won't that be a bit weird just to say it out loud for no reason?" Ollie asked.

"We probably need a code word that would be something you might say at a dinner. You know, like 'This is delicious' or 'It's incredible' or something like that," Jack said.

"Okay, how about 'Fabulous, it's fabulous,'" Luce said.

Before we could agree on a code word Molly's, Luce's and my phones all began ringing. It was each of our moms calling us. I answered to find Mom already halfway through a conversation.

"... need to chill the plate if that's going to solidify properly. Oh Harlow, finally, you answered. We're about ready so you need to get down here now," Mom said.

"What you mean, *finally* answered?" I said, but already the line had gone dead. She'd hung up on me.

My cousins appeared to have had similar conversations. Luce was scowling at her phone. Only Molly seemed relatively unaffected. She smooched Ollie on the cheek and then plucked a small piece of lint off him.

"It'll be fine. Let's go drink some wine," she rhymed again.

I saw Jack smiling to himself. He'd been present at plenty of Torrent witch disaster dinners too but he mostly thought they were funny as everything careened off the rails. I grabbed him by the arm, pulled him out the door and everyone followed along.

When we stepped inside the four men started sniffing like bloodhounds at the smell of delicious food emanating from the kitchen.

"Oh what is that? It smells like dumplings," Will said.

"Yeah, that's a dumpling, some delicious sauce," Ollie said. The four of them were so mesmerized by the scent that they hadn't noticed the dining table. Someone had put out three enormous candelabras with candles in them that were burning brightly. The lights had been turned down and so we were definitely in mood lighting for this dinner. It would have looked incredibly romantic except of course there were multiple chairs around the table and we knew we were going to have a crazy amount of people for dinner, including possibly one extra crazy costume designer. I was happy that Henry G at least was coming. I didn't know exactly what Aunt Cass's plan was but Henry G was witty and hilarious, and I'm sure would be delighted to meet the moms and to see Aunt Cass saying crazy things.

"Where is Aunt Cass?" Luce asked.

"Speak of someone fabulous and they shall appear!" Aunt Cass said from behind her.

"Ahhhh!" Luce squealed jumping in place.

Aunt Cass walked around to the head of the dining table, looking over the eight of us with an appraising eye.

"Ah, the four sets of young lovers. So glad you could bring your passionate selves to dinner," she said.

Luce and I shared a look again. It was one that said *oh no, she is definitely up to something.* Will and Ollie had plastered on faint smiles because they didn't know quite what to say. Only Jack laughed.

"So poetic this evening Cassandra," he quipped.

"That's because it is a night for love, a night for passion and poetry my darling Jack-o'-lantern," Aunt Cass said and then gave him a wink.

"Does anyone want any wine?" Luce asked, heading for the nearest bottles.

Before we could answer the three moms came bursting out of the kitchen, looking very flustered indeed.

"Oh good, everyone is almost here. Take a seat and as soon as Sheriff Hardy has arrived we'll begin," Aunt Freya said.

The moms were quickly greeting everyone when there came a knocking at the front door.

"Oh my, I wonder who that is," Aunt Cass said, barely concealing a grin.

"I assume Sheriff Hardy?" I said.

"Assume away, my fine feathered friend," Aunt Cass said and then winked at me. She pulled the door open to reveal it was in fact Sheriff Hardy, but there were two men also standing by his sides.

Behind me Mom and Aunt Freya gasped so sharply that I swear I almost felt myself get pulled back by the force of the wind.

I thought I recognized one of the men - he was the manager of the local Harlot Bay Bank. A long time ago we'd overheard that my mom had been possibly seeing the local bank manager, but we hadn't dug any further into that. If this was indeed the bank manager that she was secretly seeing invited to dinner, then that could only mean that the other man was Boris the cheesemaker, who Aunt Freya was seeing.

Both the men were in their fifties but couldn't have been dressed any more differently. The bank manager was wearing a beautiful suit and carrying what looked to be an expensive bottle of wine. The man who I assume was Boris was carrying a rough paper sack with *Dubois Cheese Company* printed on it. He was dressed in a simple pair of black pants and an open-necked blue shirt. One appeared to be a man who worked with his hands and the other one appeared to be a man who worked with other people's money. I say that in the nicest of terms because both men were trying to put on a warm face when confronted with all of us behind the doorway, staring at them.

"Come in, come in. Welcome to our dinner. Everyone, this is Varrius Dixon, bank manager and Dalilah's paramour, and this young gentleman here is Boris Dubois master cheesemaker and Freya's new love," Aunt Cass said.

There was a moment of shocked silence before Sheriff Hardy cleared his throat and gave everyone a smile.

"And me, Sheriff Hardy, who you already know," he said and came in.

"Very nice to meet you all," I said.

"I brought cheese," Boris said.

Sheriff Hardy walking in managed to pull the two other men in with him. Luce, acting on instinct, took the wine from Varrius and the cheese from Boris and gave them both glasses of white wine, which they quickly took a gulp of. I don't know what it was that Aunt Cass must've told them, but they clearly weren't expecting a gigantic family dinner.

We had a round of introductions then, Mom, Aunt Freya and Aunt Ro still somewhat frozen by the appearance of these men. I admit I got over the shock quite quickly because I was intensely curious about them. It's one thing to hear that your mom has a secret love life and it's quite another to meet the man himself. Luce for her part was looking through the bag of cheeses and then back at Boris, as though judging him by the quality of his produce.

"How did you all meet?" I asked. My question was to go unanswered because the moms finally snapped out of their daze. Mom and Aunt Freya gave Aunt Cass a look that could have killed a weaker woman. Both seemed to make a decision on the spot and then they rushed over to their respective men and smooched them right there in front of us.

"So glad you could come, I'm so happy to see you. Yes everyone, this is my paramour," Mom said, giving Varrius another kiss and Aunt Cass a glare.

"And this is Boris, who is an astounding man," Aunt Freya said, kissing him.

"Okay, okay, everyone sit down," Aunt Cass said. There was a bit of shuffling then as we all figured out where to sit. Usually between me, Molly and Luce there was a bit of a fight not to sit directly next to Aunt Cass because then you would become the buffer between her and everyone else. But surprisingly Molly volunteered for this seat and pulled Ollie down beside her.

I sat down and then Jack leaned over and whispered in my ear "What exactly is your aunt planning?" he asked.

"I have no idea. It's possible she's gone mad," I whispered back and took a sip of wine.

Barely thirty seconds had passed, people starting to make

conversation before there was another rap on the door. This time Molly jumped out of her chair.

"Oh my, who could this be now at our door? Possibly another love?" she said, dramatically. She rushed over to the door and pulled it open... only to reveal Henry G standing there holding two bottles of champagne.

"Oh, um it's Henry G, that's your name, right?" Molly said.

"Were you expecting someone else, darling?" Henry G said and swept past her.

Peta jumped up from her chair and gave him a big hug and kiss, then Henry G went around the room like he was an MC, meeting everyone and saying outrageous things. Molly closed the door and returned to her seat, sitting down to face Aunt Cass.

"Are you playing with fire, my dear?" Aunt Cass said to her.

"I guess we'll see won't we, my darling aunt," Molly said sweetly.

We made room for Henry G who quickly opened the two bottles of champagne. It wasn't long before the moms emerged from the kitchen carrying huge platters of food which they put onto the table. They had taken Boris's bag of delicious cheeses and whipped them up into an incredible platter. I recognized blue cheese, brie, camembert, and then there was a bunch of other cheeses that I had no idea what they were but they looked incredible. There was a quince paste, salami, prosciutto, black olives, green olives, artichoke hearts, cracked pepper crackers, celery, pretzels, basil pesto, some dried apricots, almonds and other nuts, a pile of grapes, figs, goat cheese, and then glistening sun-dried tomatoes in oil. That was just on one platter alone.

"Oh, that's gonna go straight to my hips," Henry G

quipped. Before anyone else could compliment that platter of food there was another knock on the door.

Molly shot up out of her seat like she was in the hundred yard dash and they had just fired the starting gun.

"Oh my, who could that be? Perhaps another lover?" she said, looking a little manic. She rushed to the door and pulled it open to reveal a man who was probably in his late sixties with gray stubble that was shaved close to the skin. He too was holding a bottle of wine and looked vaguely familiar to me.

Molly grabbed him by the arm and pulled him inside, closing the door behind him.

"Oh look who this is that I've invited to dinner tonight. This is Artemis Fogg who runs Fogg's Island Tour Company, and in keeping with the theme of this evening is Aunt Cass's paramour," Molly said.

"You can just call me Art," Art said, looking around the assorted faces, clearly confused as to what was going on.

The moms may have been shocked when Aunt Cass had invited their loves to dinner, but it was nothing compared to the expression on Aunt Cass's face now. There was a moment of shock followed by a grimace in Molly's direction and then a scrambling recovery. She leaped up from the head of the table, grabbed Art and planted a passionate kiss on his lips. When they pulled apart, the poor man was gasping.

"Yes, this is him, my lover, Art. Welcome to dinner. This is wonderful," she said. She pulled him across to the table and we all shifted down, Art taking Molly's place. There was another round of introductions, more wine and champagne poured, and then a pregnant silence as all of us looked at each other trying to work out what exactly was going on. Jack kept smiling to himself thinking this was the most hilarious thing he'd ever seen. Normally in events like this, I would feel a burst of anxiety or be worried something bad was going to happen, but for some reason I felt the same as Jack: I was laughing on the inside and just wondering what it was that Aunt Cass had planned.

The moms quickly returned to the kitchen and brought out more food. There was a platter of candied tomatoes on basil leaves and also some crispy bocconcini with a tomato chili sauce, and it turned out Will and Ollie's noses had been correct: there were a variety of dumplings served with a delicious dipping sauce. Given the moms had arrived home quite late, I honestly had no idea how they'd managed to make so much extraordinary food in such a short time. I was still personal training with Kaylee Osterman when I could, but with all this food in front of me I sent my deepest apologies to my thighs and dived in along with everyone else. In between bites I saw Molly lean over to Aunt Cass.

"Revenge is a dish best served cold," she said.

"We'll see about that," Aunt Cass said back in an undertone.

"Never send to know for whom the bell tolls: it tolls for thee," Molly said.

"What are you doing?" I whispered to Molly.

"Don't you remember, when she cursed me to only say nice things about her? Well, this is my evening of revenge," she said.

"I'm not sure inviting the guy that Aunt Cass is seeing to dinner exactly counts as revenge," I whispered.

"Revenge!" Molly declared and stabbed a dumpling.

"How did you even know Aunt Cass was inviting the moms' boyfriends anyway?"

"Saw Aunt Cass going into the bank a few days ago. Looked in the window and saw her talking with the bank manager. Put two and two together and it added up to a delicious opportunity for payback!"

The moms returned to the kitchen and brought out more

platters of food: small ravioli served with a sauce, salad, and all our guests were eating not realizing this was just the entrée and there was still the main coming. The moms finally sat down after bringing out jugs of green tea that had ginger and mint in them. I had a quick taste and it was delicious, but tonight everyone was drinking wine and champagne.

The conversation around the dinner table was like a surging ocean, waves of it rushing in from all directions and soon everyone was laughing and drinking.

"The plan is that we'll open a café and then we're gonna beat those *Magic Bean* people. We'll have delicious food and a musician," Luce said.

"One who is scruffy, very scruffy, the scruffiest musician there is, with blue eyes, incredibly blue eyes," Molly said.

"We could supply you with some delicious bread," Aunt Freya said.

"What can you tell me about the flour that bread is made with?" Luce said, waving a glass of wine that she'd perhaps had a little too much of.

"Um, it's flour and we use it to make bread," Aunt Freya said, clearly confused.

"No, no, no, no, no. That's not going to do at all. Is it stone-ground or something? Does it come from the Scottish Highlands?" Luce said, taking another drink of wine.

"I'm not sure where it comes from exactly," Aunt Freya said.

"Then we don't want it! We need bespoke! We need flour with a story! With a history! We need to tell a story with every ingredient that we're going to use in our café so we can beat those *Magic Bean* sons of... I mean *Magic Bean* people," Luce said cutting herself off.

Aunt Cass zipped away from the table at some point and returned with a variety of chili sauces, which he placed down in the center of the table.

"These aren't the chili sauces that caused that problem are they?" Mom asked, wary.

"Don't worry *these* are not *those*. These are delicious ones that everyone should try," Aunt Cass said. She dipped a dumpling in the chili sauce and then gave it to Art who ate it off her fork and then smiled back at her.

The dinner continued, the conversation surging. Ollie talked about how he was putting the posts that he'd been writing on his website together into a book of local history and then how he might publish it online for people to buy. That led to me talking about how I'd started writing a story about a ghost, and how I wasn't going to be doing much on the Harlot Bay Reader anymore. At this, Boris piped up.

"It's always good to do what you're passionate about. When I was young, I went into working in the law because that's what my father did. I even became a lawyer, but then one day I realized it wasn't for me and so I changed careers and now I make cheeses and I couldn't be happier. You need to find what makes you happy," he said, beaming across at me.

"Thanks, that makes me feel a lot better," I said to him.

Aunt Freya wrapped her arms around Boris and gave him a kiss on the cheek.

It certainly felt the night was in some crazy overload. Since our respective three fathers had left, we'd never really seen our mothers in any other role other than being mothers. Although we suspected there had been men involved, we'd never seen any at the house and apart from Aunt Ro getting together with Sheriff Hardy we had no real idea about our moms' love lives at all. Seeing them here in front of us was quite odd but there felt something quite right about it. It was as though there had been something missing from our lives for all these years.

"So Varrius, tell us an exciting banking story," Aunt Cass said, dinging her glass with her fork.

Everyone focused their attention on Varrius who coughed and then took a big gulp of wine.

I noticed he had taken off his tie at some point and now had undone the top button of his shirt as he relaxed.

"There are no exciting banking stories. It's banking, what can we say? We had someone drop a small gold bar once in the bank and then it was lost for all of four hours. Wow, what an exciting tale," he said with a smile on his face. We all laughed, although it wasn't an entertaining story, the alcohol and the night certainly helping us along.

The conversation swirled around for a while as we ate before the moms returned to the kitchen and brought out the main course. The entrées had been quite exquisite but the mains they brought out looked like regular burgers at first glance.

"Buffalo turkey burgers with blue cheese, lettuce and broccolini slaw served with a side salad," Aunt Ro announced.

They quickly served out the burgers and everyone dug in although we were full from the entrées.

"Oh I have died and gone to food heaven," Henry G said.

I bit into my burger and groaned myself. It was utterly delectable.

"This is the type of thing you should serve at the café," I said to Molly and Luce.

"Burgers for all!" Luce shouted out, definitely having had a little too much wine.

I took a quick trip to the bathroom and when I returned I touched Art on the shoulder as I moved by him. There was a sudden burst of sound, seagulls and ropes creaking, the sound of people talking and laughing, the gentle lapping of waves. It came and went in a moment. It was Art's history, his life I guessed. I sat down in my chair, smiling to myself and feeling quite good. Honestly, it was rare that a Slip witch power turned out to be positive rather than negative. Feeling a little tipsy, the next time Boris reached out to grab some food, I did too and brushed my fingers against his hand. I heard cows mooing, sheep and goats bleating, and the sound of laughter. I tried again when Varrius reached for the last dumpling. This time I heard noise of a typewriter clacking away. Clack, clack, clack, ding. Behind it I faintly heard the sound of coins dropping onto a marble floor.

"Are you okay?" Jack whispered to me.

I realized I was smiling like an idiot.

"Yes, I am far, far better than okay," I said.

Somehow the conversation swirled around back to the play and then to Hans being poisoned (which had since been confirmed by Sheriff Hardy).

"He's still in the hospital and it's both good and bad news. Because he didn't die there's a good chance he'll survive but because he's still unconscious it's not looking great. I can't say much more," Sheriff Hardy said.

There was a moment of silence then as the night had turned abruptly serious.

"Fabulous!" Molly blurted out, using the code word.

"So was I led to believe that there was some big news for tonight?" I said, trying to change the topic away from possible poisoning and attempted murder.

"Well, yes, there is actually," Aunt Ro said. She interlinked her arm with Sheriff Hardy and everyone grew quiet, bringing their attention back onto the sheriff. He looked around the room at family members, boyfriends, half-brother, friends and our crazy guest Henry G, and then gave us all a soft smile.

"We'd like to announce that we are going to get married," he said.

The sudden squealing and celebration from all the Torrent witches took all of the men by surprise. I swear Boris, Varrius, and Art nearly fell out of their chairs. Only Henry G went with it, jumping up and clapping and yelling as though he had known us his whole life. Aunt Ro and Sheriff Hardy were enveloped by witches, hugging them and kissing, and talking all at once. I got around the other side of the table so fast I felt like I teleported there.

Eventually Aunt Ro and Sheriff Hardy fought their way free and we all returned to our seats, still talking at high speed.

"When's the wedding going to be? Have you set a date?" Aunt Freya said.

"It's going to be in two weeks," Aunt Ro said.

This set off another explosion of conversation, Mom and Aunt Freya going between complete excitement and sudden terror because how could they possibly arrange a wedding within two weeks?

Aunt Cass was standing at the head of the dinner table grinning to herself.

"What are you so happy about?" I called out over the noise.

"This couldn't be more perfect. Exactly what I wanted," she said, looking around it all the assembled guests.

We quieted a down a bit and kept eating. Aunt Cass dinged her wine glass to focus all the attention on her and then pointed a finger at Luce and Mollie.

"When are you two going to get married? Or are you going to go and get pregnant first and then get married like some other Torrents that I know," she said.

"Aunt Cass!" Aunt Ro gasped.

"That is not true at all," Mom said, talking to me, Molly and Luce.

"All three of us were married when you were born," Aunt Freya said primly.

"Barely," Aunt Cass said.

"Oh my goddess, really?" Luce said, staring at her mother.

"I'd check the marriage dates and the birth dates if I were you."

"When were you married Mom?" Luce demanded.

"Oh, don't listen to her, she's just trying to stir up trouble," Aunt Freya snapped.

"Perhaps we can get our librarian here to research some dates and see if they match up," Aunt Cass said. She turned her attention to Molly.

"So is that your plan, pregnancy and then a marriage or are you going to get married and then get pregnant?"

"Well, why don't you tell me what you and Art are going to do. Planning on getting married? A spring wedding perhaps? Is it common that you marry your little piece of fluff on the side?" Molly sniped, the conversation careening off.

"Fabulous! Fabulous!" I shouted out.

This time it was Peta and Jonas who jumped in. "Jonas is currently redeveloping the governor's mansion. He's been looking into that haven't you Jonas?" Peta said. Everyone looked across at Jonas, who was in the spotlight.

"Um yeah, we're looking into it, but we're being blocked. I… I think it's Coldwell actually," he said. At the sound of his name there were a few scowls from around the dinner table, particularly from Jack, Sheriff Hardy and me. Coldwell was a bad man who did bad things but seemed to get away with it constantly. The last we'd heard of him he had been thrown out of control of Sunny Days Manor which he'd been apparently running down into the ground in an attempt to make a lowball offer to buy out the silent partners. A few men who'd been working for him had been arrested after being caught trying to burn part of the manor down to ensure the deal went through. But they'd all refused to speak or implicate Coldwell.

"How is he blocking you?" Molly asked, distracted from fencing with Aunt Cass.

"I think maybe he has contacts with people who are in power. Or something else is happening," Jonas said, choosing his words carefully. I knew exactly what he wanted to say: "I think he's bribing people."

Seeing his half-brother's discomfort, Jack picked up the baton.

"Harlow and I are going to Arlan and Hilda's wedding which should be fun. I heard the ice-skating rink has opened up again so we might go there as well," he said.

We all started talking again and soon the moms returned to the kitchen and returned with dessert which was, again, absolutely exquisite. There was a triple chocolate biscotti, a soft coconut lime ball, and then a chocolate pudding served with a home-made vanilla ice-cream. As we were eating Jack touched me again on the arm and this time there was a burst of sound. I heard wood sawing, hammering, the sounds of building but then behind it I could hear Jack telling someone in a firm voice to lay on the ground, to put their hands behind their head. I heard him talking to someone else, a male voice, saying that they had to keep up observation and that soon he would slip up. It came and went in a moment, leaving me feeling... comforted actually. It felt good to hear my partner's past, to listen to what he was now. I wondered if I could hear myself? Would it be me typing away trying to write the Harlot Bay Reader, or perhaps the noise of me getting involved in crazy supernatural things that seem to happen around Harlot Bay?

I was musing on this and listening to the chatter of multiple different conversations at once when I felt a furry presence by my leg. It was Adams and he had his bowtie in his mouth again. He dropped it next to my foot.

"Put it on and I want some cheese too," he whispered. I took a quick guilty look around but everyone was too wrapped up in their conversations to notice Adams under the table so I reached down, clipped the bowtie around his neck, and then grabbed a chunk of blue cheese, which I gave to him. He took it gently in his mouth rather than gobbling it down, which was odd, and then carried it off, quickly stepping behind the darkness of the table leg and vanishing off to who knows where.

Was he just keeping that cheese somewhere? What was going on?

We kept eating and talking, Sheriff Hardy and Aunt Ro's wedding being the main topic of conversation. I noticed Aunt Cass kept looking down at something in her hand and when I glanced over I saw it was a small piece of fabric with a line drawn across it. When Art excused himself to go to the bathroom I moved over to his chair.

"What are you looking at that for, is it a spell?" I asked.

I already knew the answer, of course. The magic always swirled around us and I could feel it near the piece of fabric.

"I don't think it worked," Aunt Cass said.

Her previous glee seemed to have drained away.

"What's the spell for?" I whispered.

"I was trying to catch something but it didn't work," Aunt Cass said. Art soon returned and I had to move back to my chair but soon she called out to me.

"How many people are coming to Hilda and Arlan's wedding?" she asked.

"We're sitting on table forty so I think it's a lot," I said.

"Yeah that might work," Aunt Cass said to herself. In any other moment, and perhaps if we didn't have so many people around I would have pursued that, but the wine and the chocolate and the meal were making me feel euphoric and not worried about too many things.

This lovely, joyful, feeling that had been spread across the table was broken by most horrible squawking and squealing noise outside. There was the sound of cracking and piercing shrieks.

We all rushed outside into the dark to discover about fifty birds swirling around in the air having an vicious fight. They were dive-bombing each other, pecking, and screeching at the top of their lungs. It wasn't just seagulls but other local birds as well. There was even a duck in there, larger than most of them, viciously pulling smaller birds out of the air and flinging them to the ground.

"What is going on? This is crazy," Ollie said aloud.

I saw Aunt Cass give the moms a look and then Aunt Cass pointed into the distance. "What's that over there everyone? Oh my goddess, is that causing it?" she shouted out. All of the men turned their attention to where Aunt Cass was pointing. From behind us I felt a surge of a spell from the moms and then a great wind came gusting around the corner of the mansion, picking up speed as it went, lifting up dirt and bits of stone. It hit the birds who scattered, squealing in protest. Within a few moments they were gone. The only sign that they'd been there was the ground littered in feathers and droplets of blood.

There were another one of those silences but this one seemed to stretch out forever. The night was definitely over.

"Chika cha!" Molly said and looked around at us but no one had anything to say that could rescue the night from what had just happened.

CHAPTER SIX

"*I* think we should try the push-up bra," Luce said, studying me with a calculated eye.

"No I think she has enough cleavage. I read an article that told me you shouldn't have more than a credit card size worth of cleavage or it's just too much," Molly said. She grabbed her purse off the table and pulled out a credit card. I managed to fend her off.

"Stop it. You're not going to put that in my cleavage," I said, pushing her away.

"This is science Harlow," Molly said, but then put the credit card back in her purse. It was the day after our giant ridiculous dinner and Harlot Bay had put on spectacular weather for Arlan and Hilda's wedding. I was wearing a simple sundress with flowers on it but the way my cousins were behaving you would have thought it was *my* wedding. Luce was on the side of 'show some more leg, show some more cleavage.' Molly, although she wanted it more demure, was going crazy in her own way.

I checked the time. Jack was a little late but we still had

plenty of time to make it to the wedding, which was being held in the Harlot Bay Botanic Gardens.

Luce dashed off to her room and returned with a push-up bra. Before she could try to wrangle me into it Jack's truck pulled up outside so she stuffed it down the back of the sofa.

Jack's truck is a work truck. He's usually carrying around bits of lumber and inside it smells of old leather and wood shavings. So it was slightly incongruous to see him open the door and step out wearing a perfectly cut suit and white shirt.

The three of us gasped.

"Oh, Harlow, you need to put a ring on that," Molly said.

"Do you think we can hire him to stand in the corner of our new café?" Luce said.

"Va va voom," I said.

Jack walked up to the front door, gave a brief knock and then opened it to find the three of us standing there like stunned fish with our mouths open.

"Ladies," he said by way of greeting and then winked at us.

"You look like a secret agent," I said. Jack swept me into his arms and gave me a kiss that left my knees quivering.

"This old thing? It was just something I threw on," he said. He checked the time.

"We've got to go or we're going to be late," he said.

"Are you sure you don't play the guitar Jack?" Molly asked, not for the first time.

"Still having trouble finding someone scruffy with blue eyes?"

"They're just not *scruffy* enough is the problem," Luce complained.

"I wonder if Ollie has a suit," I heard Molly murmur as Jack grabbed me by the hand and pulled me out the door. We were driving down the hill and I just kept touching his arm, feeling the suit and the firm muscle beneath it.

"You look beautiful," he said to me with a grin.

"Are you sure? Luce thinks I should have worn a push-up bra so I have more cleavage," I said, shuffling things up a little bit.

Jack laughed and shook his head. "I think you've just got the right amount," he said with a devilish sideways grin.

We bounced along down the road hitting a few potholes that had yet to be filled. Although I know my cousins were going a little bit crazy this morning and pretending this was my wedding rather than Hilda's, I had a very odd feeling that it kind of almost *was* my wedding. Jack was in a suit. I was in a dress. I was deeply in love with him and he was deeply in love with me. Would this be what it was like?

I went into ten seconds of daydreaming before Jack pulled me out of it.

"So did you find out what was happening with those birds? And what Aunt Cass might've been doing?" he asked.

"Nope, Aunt Cass wouldn't tell me, and after I asked her again she went storming down to the basement and magically sealed the door so no one could follow her. She's been in a mood all morning," I said.

"So she went and locked herself in her 'lair'," Jack said, making the air quote marks with his fingers.

"Yeah, I guess so. I wish she'd just talk to us and tell the truth sometimes," I said.

As soon as the sentence left my mouth I felt a stab of guilt. I'd sworn some time ago to tell the truth, to always be open, to not lie no matter how scary it was. But there had been one thing I simply hadn't been able to tell Jack. I hadn't been able to say to him that I had a "lair" of my own. Even when I went into it, it looked crazy. This gigantic wall of newspaper cuttings and maps and bits of string. Another wall with notes about John Smith. He'd taken me and my family being witches incredibly well, taken it in his stride you might say, but it felt like a crazy cottage might be a step too far. Sometimes I realized that my reluctance was perhaps the spell that was potentially cast on me pushing me not to tell him, and although I had moments where I'd resolved to tell the truth, to say it out loud, they always passed quickly. This was one of those times.

We arrived in town just in time for me to see John Smith hurl himself off another tall building in the center of town. As usual, he hit the ground and then stood up, looking disappointed.

"Do you see something?" Jack said.

"John stuck in his loop doing the same thing over and over again," I said.

We drove through town which was reasonably busy for this time of morning and a weekend. It was between seasons where the tourist numbers were slowly building up, heading towards summer when the streets would be so clogged it was sometimes better just to park the car and walk rather than drive around Harlot Bay. As my mind strayed off the lair that I was keeping secret, I realized I hadn't told Jack about my new Slip witch power.

"Quickly changing the topic, I think I'm hearing things about people now," I began. As we drove through town I quickly described what happened when I touched Henry G, the sounds I'd heard of a frog and Shakespearean insults and someone shouting. I told him how I'd listened to the sound of sawing and hammers and then conversations about police matters when I touched him. Jack listened to me with a slight look of amazement on his face.

"That's an extraordinary thing," he said. "Did you go downstairs to touch your grandma to see if you could hear anything?" he asked.

"No, I hadn't even thought of that!" I said.

How could I have not thought of that? It seemed so obvious! My excitement was quickly dampened however when I remembered that this new power didn't have a hundred percent success rate and that I'd touched people and hadn't heard anything at all.

"I wonder what would happen if I grabbed Aunt Cass on the arm," I mused.

We pulled up outside the Harlot Bay Botanic Gardens in one of last few free car parking spaces.

"Maybe you would hear her doing some roadwork around the town, or perhaps plumbing?" Jack said.

"What are you talking about?" I said as we got out of the truck.

"Have a look over there," he said. There down the street on the edge of the Botanic Gardens in the distance was a familiar figure. It was Aunt Cass dressed in coveralls, a bright yellow hardhat, and it looked like she had a belt of tools around her waist. She also had that rock climbing rope slung over her shoulder again. As we watched, she knelt down next to a tree and did something before standing up and walking away, quickly vanishing.

"Do you think we should follow her?" Jack asked.

I checked the time. The wedding was due to start in a couple of minutes. Although I was burning with curiosity as to what exactly she was doing, I shook my head.

"No, let's go to the wedding. We can come back later and see what she was doing if it's still there," I said.

We walked into the gardens and followed the sound of voices. We quickly found around three hundred people standing in a group, some of them milling around. Children were running and laughing and playing. There were rows and rows of white chairs set out on the green grass, leading to a floral arch and a dais where a priest stood wearing his gowns.

"Is this how you imagined it would be?" Jack asked, looking sideways at me.

"Hilda's wedding? Is that what you mean?" I said.

"No, I mean *your* wedding. Adams told me that you had a scrapbook you made when you were a teenager," Jack said, teasing me.

"That little sneak needs to stop blabbing my secrets," I said.

"What can I say? I'm used to interrogating suspects and Adams likes to hang out in the rubble and also enjoys tuna," Jack said.

"Okay you want the answer, Mr. Fancy Suit – yes, I've considered a garden wedding, but I've also considered a beach wedding. I'm not sure yet. Perhaps when I find someone to marry, I'll be able to decide," I said.

Jack flinched and put a hand up over his heart. "Ouch, oh that was cold," he said, laughing.

I punched him in the arm and then as we stood there laughing the violinists at the front began to play. People quickly found their seats although there were a bunch of us that remained standing. Apparently, there hadn't been enough white chairs for every guest. We stood on the left-hand side of the aisle and watched the wedding. First, two adorable little flower girls, most likely great-granddaughters I assume, came running up the aisle scattering petals across the grass. They were followed by Eve, Hilda's granddaughter who looked stunning in a pale blue dress, her dark hair plaited and curled around her neck. She gave me a smile as she walked by. Next up the aisle came Arlan dressed in a black suit and beaming with joy. The last time I'd seen him, he'd been in hospital after jumping off the Harlot Bay light-house and breaking a leg. He'd done that because he'd been compelled by the Shadow Witch who had taken over his body. Now he looked healthy and happy, and there was no sign of the magical strife he had gotten into. I expected I'd be happy when I saw him, but I also felt a sudden prickle of tears. I'd saved his life with my magic, stopping him hitting the ground as hard as he would have and now it seemed an enormous, ridiculous thing. If I hadn't been there in time, this day would not exist, this moment would not be happening. For an absurd instant it felt like I was separated from a terrible alternate universe by the thinnest of bubbles, and if I pushed too hard I might accidentally slip into it, into one where I had failed to save him, and the park would be empty, with me just standing on the grass, looking around and feeling sad. The moment came and went, and because there were plenty of people around us with tears in their own eyes I blended in quite well as I wiped mine away. Following behind Arlan was his best man, another man in his late eighties with a shock of white hair and a roguish smile. Arlan and his best man stood at the front, and for a moment, I swear I could see what they would have looked like when they were young, grinning at the girls and winning all kinds of favors with their cheeky smiles. Soon, Hilda came walking up the aisle. She was wearing a white wedding dress, but much shorter than usual and there was no long train carrying on behind it. She was carrying a bunch of flowers with brilliant blue petals rimmed in red. I had no idea what they were but Hilda had worked in botany and science in her life, so I was sure that they were some unusual breed of flower that she had chosen just for this occasion. She reached the front and then there was that expectant pause, that divine moment with everyone waiting.

Jack leaned down and whispered in my ear, "Maybe one day we should do this," he said. I felt a burst of goosebumps over my body. I wanted to shout out *yes!* as though that had been a wedding proposal. I just squeezed his arm and rested my head on his shoulder.

He turned towards me and for some reason I expected him to whisper something romantic again, but it wasn't to be.

"Your aunt is over there in the trees," he whispered.

I looked out through the floral gate and sure enough, there was Aunt Cass in the trees, fiddling with something.

"Oh goddess, please don't let her disrupt this wedding," I whispered.

"She wouldn't do that would she?" Jack whispered to me.

"I honestly don't know," I said.

The priest started speaking, introducing the couple and talking about what marriage was, but I was only half listening. Aunt Cass finished whatever she was doing and then I saw her moving across between the trees before ducking down to do something again. I had an intense urge to sneak out of the wedding and go into the trees to find out what she was doing. I took a quick look around seeing everyone was focused on the priest, the bride, and her husband-to-be. I looked back to the forest but Aunt Cass was gone. I suspected she was hiding somewhere or had cast a concealment spell possibly.

While the priest spoke I took a few deep breaths and allowed myself to feel the magic that was swirling around me. Today the magic was calm, a serene lapping, like gentle waves on the shore. Because we were in a garden, I could feel the plants and trees around me catching hints of memories of happy times, picnics and children running and laughing. I let my awareness expand outwards until finally I felt the faint edge of something, another type of spell behind the tree line. From where I was I couldn't quite detect what it was, but it was all the confirmation I needed. Aunt Cass had cast a spell out there and was doing something.

I snapped back to the here and now as the couple exchanged rings and then kissed, the wedding ceremony quickly over. I joined everyone cheering and clapping and yes, the moment was incredibly happy but somewhere in my stomach, anxiety bubbled. Aunt Cass hadn't disrupted the wedding but yet again, there was something going on. She'd been up to something last night too at the dinner, inviting the moms' boyfriends along and even though she appeared shocked when Molly had invited Art, she had said that it fit perfectly in her plan.

The assorted wedding guests moved away from the makeshift aisle and over to an area to the side where there were benches crowded with platters of food and a large tent filled with tables and chairs. As Hilda and Arlan signed their wedding certificates, everyone gathered and mingled, eating food and starting to open bottles of champagne. Waiters in white shirts and black pants began to circulate carrying bottles of wine and trays of glasses.

"I'm going to quickly sneak off to the trees to see if I can find anything," I said to Jack.

"I'll come with you," Jack said.

We turned to find a beaming Amaris standing there, the girl from the play who'd told the three boys to steal something for her to prove their love. She was dressed in black pants and white shirt and was carrying a tray full of wine glasses. Beside her was a teenage boy I didn't know, carrying bottles of champagne.

"Harlow, you look beautiful! Would you like some champagne?" Amaris said.

"No, I think we're okay," I said, glancing over her shoulder. I caught a flash of yellow hard hat between the trees. Aunt Cass was going back picking up whatever she had put down.

"It's delicious," Amaris said, smiling at me. "We should

have something like this at our cast party when we finish the play. Isn't that crazy about those sandbags?" she said. Seeing we weren't going to be able to get away quickly, Jack grabbed two glasses of champagne off the tray and handed one to me.

"Thank you so much for the champagne but we have to talk to someone over there right now," he said and gave Amaris a charming smile.

The poor girl didn't know what hit her. I swear her knees went weak and she blushed from the tip of her toes to the top of her head. She mumbled something, possibly about blue eyes, and I saw the teenage boy next to her scowl at Jack. He grabbed my arm and hauled me off, leaving Amaris standing there somewhat starstruck.

I quickly downed my glass of champagne, which was quite delicious, and Jack did the same before quickly depositing the glasses on an empty tray that another teenager was carrying around. We were moving away from the gathering, heading for the treeline where there was only scattered guests when one of them called out.

"Harlow, so happy to see you!"

It was Eve. She said goodbye to the guest she was talking to and rushed over. I was glad to see her, but my heart sank. I could see Aunt Cass's yellow hardhat moving through the forest. She was faster now, whatever it was she was doing.

I couldn't be rude to Eve, so we had a few moments of chitchatting about the wedding, about the weather and how amazing it was before she said goodbye and rushed off to talk to other people. We quickly walked off into the treeline and I found the tree that I thought Aunt Cass had been meddling with something behind.

"Anything there?" Jack asked.

"No, whatever it is, it's gone," I said. I could feel a faint imprint of magic. There had been something there but whatever it was Aunt Cass had taken it.

"She's over there," Jack said, pointing through the trees into the distance.

We rushed off, away from the wedding and cross-country through the Botanic Gardens. Aunt Cass was out on the street and had set up traffic cones before pulling a manhole cover up and climbing down into it. I called out but she either ignored or didn't hear me. We ended up betting blocked by a low hedge and had to find a way around it, and by the time we made our way to the traffic cones and the open manhole, Aunt Cass was gone.

"Are we going down there?" Jack asked me.

"Your suit is too beautiful. What if we ruin it?" I asked.

"Well we can take our clothes off and go down in our underwear, but I'm not sure how that's going to look," Jack said. I looked around and saw there were still a few people in the street, so quickly cast a concealment spell over Jack and me. It pulled on me quite sharply as though someone had just thrown a twenty-pound bag of concrete at me and expected me to catch it.

"Go now," I urged Jack.

He climbed down the small rusty ladder and I followed, letting the concealment spell go as soon as we were both underground. Halfway down the ladder I let light go from my palm. We climbed down the ladder into the sewer system of Harlot Bay. I say sewer system, which sounds gross, but it was just stormwater drains. They smelt of dirt and wet and mold.

At the bottom, there was no sign of Aunt Cass but somewhere in the distance we could hear a tapping sound of footsteps and something splashing.

"Let's go aunt hunting," Jack said.

I let the light drift up above us. We walked along the narrow concrete pathway that was beside a deep flow of dark water. It hadn't been raining much but apparently whatever water had been coming down was enough to make a fast moving current. In it there were small sticks and also some bits of rubbish that had been washed down into the stormwater drains. As we walked we passed open archways that led off in other directions and then there was even a set of stairs that went further down and another ladder.

"I bet Ollie would love to come down here to see some of this," Jack said, pointing at some etchings on the wall.

"Provided he can get down here when it isn't raining and is unlikely to drown," I said. Sometime in the past some people had etched their initials and a date (1872) into the wall.

We kept moving following the sound of footsteps, until eventually we turned a corner and there she was, Aunt Cass in her coveralls and her hardhat, a light hovering above her shoulder. She tied a rope to an iron grill on the wall which was connected to her belt, and she was leaning out over the water with a long stick with a glass tube on the end of it.

"Don't stand there gawking, give me another one of those test tubes," she said.

I walked up and saw she had an open toolbox full of small glass vials.

"This is so super dangerous. What are you doing?" I said.

"I have a rope, it's not dangerous at all," Aunt Cass argued. She scooped up some water in the test tube and then turned to hand it to me. She gave me a small rubber cork that she had been holding in one hand. I quickly pressed the cork into the test tube and then gave her an empty one from the box. She used it to get another sample and then she used the rope to pull herself back in so she wasn't leaning out over the water.

Once she had put the rubber cork in place, she looked us over.

"Quite well dressed for a trip into the storm drains aren't we?" she said.

"Well you know how it is Cass. A suit is perfect for weddings or hunting down aunts doing magical things," Jack said with a twinkle in his eye.

"I'm not doing anything illegal in case that policeman sense of yours is tingling," she said.

"Do you want to explain what it is you are doing because you were just up there outside that wedding doing something magical and now you're down here collecting water samples. And I'm fairly sure last night you invited all those people for some reason connected to this," I said.

Aunt Cass shrugged and put the water samples back into her toolbox.

"You, James Bond, carry that. You get the ropes," she instructed. Jack picked up the toolbox and I gathered the ropes.

"Let's get out of this place," she said.

We walked back, heading to the surface our lights bobbing along above us.

"No, seriously, you need to tell us what you're doing," I said after a minute of silence.

"*Cryptobranchus amarebelle* is what I'm doing. It's a magical salamander," Aunt Cass said.

"You mean those little lizard things?" I said.

"Twenty dollars to the girl in the floral dress," Aunt Cass said. "I suspect that one has come to town. This particular species cause feelings of love when they're small. It seeps from their skin. It causes people and animals and anything alive really to experience feelings of love, which it then feeds from. It absorbs this love and grows bigger. But it's never enough. The love gets more intense and then you get more fights, more problems, eventually leading to violence. The salamander grows, feeding on these emotions and amplifying

73

until eventually you end up with hatred and death. At that point the salamander will lay its eggs and go into hibernation for a few decades."

We climbed the ladder, Aunt Cass emerging into the light and then casting a quick concealment spell over Jack and me who, in our suit and dress, looked like we definitely shouldn't be down in the water system. We walked a little away from where Aunt Cass was as she heaved the manhole cover back into place and then collected the traffic cones, all of which I noticed were inscribed with Harlot Bay Traffic Authority. Once she had gathered them Aunt Cass waved us over to the side of the Botanic Gardens and took a seat on a park bench there. She waved Jack over with the toolbox, which she opened, and rummaged around in until she found a set of small plastic strips.

"So you think one of these - what did you call it? Crypto-branchus what now? You think one is in town?"

"Its common name is the Love and War Salamander, and yes, I was doing something... and I thought I detected it. Seeing as it's going to be a problem for the town and inter-fere with other things, we need to catch it," Aunt Cass said.

She had paused in the middle, about to blurt out what she'd been doing but then covered it up. But I hadn't missed it, and neither had Jack.

"What is it you're investigating Cassandra? You know, the more people who work on an investigation, usually the faster it goes. We can help you," Jack said.

Aunt Cass gave me a sharp look that seemed to say "you should have kept everything secret" but then her face softened.

"Let's just focus on the salamander first," she said to Jack. She took out the small glass vials, opened them, and then dipped the strips into them. The first one turned a pale pink instantly. The second one stayed clear, but then, as we stood there watching, slowly turned brown. Aunt Cass sealed the water back up and put it back into the toolbox.

"So what is this meant to mean? What are the pink and brown strips?" I asked.

"One is measuring the amount of, basically, love, the substance that's in the water. The other one is measuring what you would call war, how much conflict it's going to produce. From this, I'd say it's about one quarter grown," Aunt Cass said.

A sudden thought struck me and I understood exactly what had been going on last night.

"It's attracted to places of high emotions isn't it, where there's a lot of love and conflict and things like that? That's why you had the dinner put on and that's why you invited the moms' new boyfriends, and that's why you weren't upset that Art came," I said. I may have taken it a little too far because I practically leaped on the spot and pointed my finger at her as though I was a judge bringing down a sentence.

"Oh yes, brilliant, you figured it out. Now here, take these," Aunt Cass said, handing me a bunch of test strips.

"What am I meant to do with these?" I said.

"You're going to share them with your cousins and then I'm going to give you a map of all the storm drains across Harlot Bay and you're going to go down into them, take a sample of water and test it and tell me what color it is and how saturated. Hopefully we'll be able to discover where the salamander has its nest before it moves to the final stage and we get blood on the streets," Aunt Cass said in a very sarcastic tone as though it was incredibly obvious what it was I should be doing.

"I do have a life you know. I have things to do other than going down into drains to take water samples," I said.

"I know you do, darling, but other people have a life too

and if we want to keep them having lives, we need to find the salamander," she said.

"I'll help. We can do it together," Jack said.

"So what was it you were doing behind the trees, though?" I asked. I handed Jack the test strips because my dress didn't have any pockets.

"I thought Hilda's wedding might attract it with so many people and such a large dose of love. So I set up a trap of sorts. I thought at least I could mark the salamander if it appeared and trace it back to its nest. But it didn't work; nothing came. Just the same as last night. I don't know, maybe something is interfering with it," Aunt Cass said with a frown.

I remembered the birds last night fighting like crazy, pecking, feathers fluttering down with droplets of blood on them.

"So those birds last night, was that love or war?"

Aunt Cass stood up, gathered her tools, her rope, and the traffic cones.

"Who said there was a difference?" she said and gave both of us a wink before walking away down the street.

CHAPTER SEVEN

"Snitches get stitches. Pass me that plate," Mom instructed, turning the bacon.

"I'm not snitching! I just think it's important that you and Aunt Freya and Aunt Ro are aware that Aunt Cass is going down into the stormwater system to collect water samples to track down a magical salamander!" I said.

"Plate please. Besides, we already know," Mom said. I passed her the serving plate and she piled it high with bacon. From the main dining room came the hubbub of guests who had all arrived yesterday at the last minute. There were at least twenty of them and they had booked every room in the Torrent mansion, some of them sleeping on the floors of the bedrooms. They'd arrived yesterday in a giant orange bus, which was now parked in front of the mansion.

"Well if you already know about it then it's not snitching," I said.

The morning certainly wasn't going the way I thought it would. I'd been downstairs to touch Grandma on the arm but hadn't heard a sound so that was a bust. I had to go to rehearsal soon but I thought I'd talk to mom or whoever else might be around about the job that Aunt Cass had laid on us. Yesterday after Jack and I had returned from the wedding, we'd come home to find a map of stormwater drains sitting on the kitchen table, a pile of magical testing sticks, as well as instructions from Aunt Cass, giving us dates and times. Molly and Luce had arrived home from seeing Will and Ollie, and then I had to explain to them what Aunt Cass had told me about the salamander. We tried to find Aunt Cass but she'd been nowhere to be found that evening, and we had to stop looking when the busload of guests had arrived, piling out of the orange bus like they'd been stuffed in there like sardines. My plan had been to come down in the morning, talk to Mom or whoever else, and see if we could get some family help on this salamander problem, only to find out that they already knew and were apparently completely fine with us traipsing around the stormwater drains.

"Don't you think it's just the slightest bit dangerous," I said, still quite miffed.

Mom started flipping eggs with expert speed.

"Well yes, it is a little dangerous, but we need to catch that salamander. At the moment not much can happen, but as it grows and absorbs more of the emotional energy things could turn quite dangerous. As local witches it's our responsibility to intervene," Mom said. She reached the end of a row of eggs and started going back in the other direction flipping them.

For some reason I couldn't let it go.

"I'm going to be down in the stormwater drain, leaning out over those waters with a glass tube collecting and then testing it and maybe could get swept away in a wash of water. That's okay?" I said.

Mom finished flipping all the eggs and then grabbed a serving dish and began pulling them off the grill.

"Yes, darling, it's fine," she said. "Now take that bacon out to the table and then come back for the eggs," she instructed. I grabbed the gigantic platter of bacon, wiped the disgruntled look off my face and went out to the main dining room. Every chair was full of guests who were talking excitedly. A woman in the middle with fiery red hair waved her arm at me and pointed to put the bacon in front of her.

"Nice to meet you, I'm Galina," she called out over the noise.

"Harlow Torrent," I said back and then put the plate of bacon down. She offered her hand and I shook it. I heard a sudden rush of noise, much like the noise around me but it was people chanting something. It sounded like "No, no, it has to go".

It came and went in a flash and I gave Galina a smile before returning to the kitchen to grab the plates full of eggs that Mom had cooked. I spent the next five minutes ferrying food out to the table before Mom finally released me from servitude and I left to go to rehearsals at the theater.

I rushed back to my end of the mansion and had a quick shower, ate another piece of toast and made sure I had a change of clothes in my bag. Tonight was a part-time at the library night where I'd be sorting papers into piles again and I was sure to get dusty.

By the time I got ready I saw I was going to be late if I spent any more time at home, so I rushed out, jumped in my car, and raced as fast as I could down the hill, noticing that the orange tourist bus that was parked outside was now gone. Once I reached town, I stopped at some lights and I was sitting there before a shape across the road resolved itself into a poster plastered on the side of a building.

It said "See Shakespeare's most controversial play *The Taming of the Shrew* directed by Hans Holtz."

The image on the front was a picture of Kira with her

arms crossed, looking quite shrewish with Amaris, who played Bianca, in the background.

I had no idea when the pictures had been taken but they were quite good.

The light changed and I drove into town. When I rounded the corner to the theater I saw the giant orange bus parked on the street. It was when I stopped and saw the people standing outside the theater with the signs that I started to get a burbling anxiety in my stomach. One of them had a gigantic sign and written on it was "The Shrew is sexist!" with a bright red exclamation mark.

I saw Galina with her fiery hair handing out signs to the other guests who I'd only seen a short while ago eating breakfast at the Torrent mansion. None of these signs were saying anything particularly kind about the play. I got out of my car and then noticed Carter was off to the side inter-viewing one of the protesters. I grabbed my things, planning on rushing through them and going into the theater but Carter saw me and came in my direction. He had his recorder out with the light blinking, but in a change of pace for him he turned it off and stuffed it into his satchel.

"I need to talk to you, Harlow, it's urgent," he said.

I saw Galina looking at me; I think assessing if I was just coincidentally on the street or whether I was working for the play. The protesters were crowding around the entrance so I reluctantly waved Carter across to the other side of the road. Once we were away from the protesters he reached into his satchel and pulled out a piece of paper which he handed to me. I glanced over it, not taking in what I was reading. It was a memorandum from the council.

"Is this saying that something has been approved?" I said.

"Coldwell managed to get his *mall* approved yesterday afternoon in an emergency session. This is what it says, that's one of his many business names that he operates under," Carter said.

I took a couple of deep breaths and read through the paper again, my eyes finally focusing on the words. As Carter had said the council had convened in an emergency session, although it would be hard to describe exactly why voting on a proposed mall would constitute an emergency, and then had voted for it yesterday afternoon.

"Normally all council business must be notified in advance but because it was an emergency session they could do it without anyone knowing," Carter said.

I took another deep breath and let out a sigh as I heard the protesters across the road begin to chant.

It was all too familiar. I'd just heard it this morning when I'd touched Galina's hand.

"No, no it has to go," they were chanting.

"Oh goddess, this is going to be bad for everyone," I said, meaning the mall, but also partially the protesters.

"They're called *the Lanterns*. Apparently they quote 'shine a light on the dark,'" Carter said.

"So protesting a small town putting on the *Taming of the Shrew* is shining a light on the dark?" I asked.

"They don't like the play and given the posters that have appeared around town it seems that the organizers are playing off that by highlighting it's Shakespeare's most controversial work," Carter said.

We stood there for a moment silence, me watching a bunch of the teenage actors walk up the street. The protesters graciously made way but kept up their chanting and the teenagers went inside, casting looks at the protesters as they went.

"Well at least they're not stopping people entering the theater," I said.

"The play and the protesters are small news. We need to

work out what to do about Coldwell. I need you and your family to help," Carter said.

Keep in mind here folks that Carter has no idea that we're witches, or at least I don't think he does. You should also keep in mind however that I was fairly sure he referred Eve Navarro to me a few months ago when her grandmother Hilda and other elderly residents of Sunny Days Manor were going missing, apparently under the control of a supernatural force.

"What exactly am my family or I meant to do about this? I'm not even a journalist anymore. I've stopped writing for the *Harlot Bay Reader*; I'm writing a book now," I said.

That last bit surprised even me. I'd known I was writing a *story* while I was sitting in my lair, but it was news to me that I was writing a book as well. It was the second time I'd told Carter something that was true about my life that apparently I was unaware of.

"We all know that your family has been involved with the Sheriff and various crimes around town, mostly on the solving side of them. I also suspect your Aunt Cass has worked with the police in the past. I'm not going to publish any of this. Coldwell cannot build that mall. He cannot be trusted and we need to work together to take him down. He is a bad man and he will continue to do bad things," Carter said.

Carter has had it in for Coldwell since he'd evicted him and the *Harlot Bay Times* from their original location. He'd then had to move to a new location which Coldwell in a moment of spite purchased, so that he could evict Carter again.

"Where are you working from these days?" I asked.

"My home, in a room out the back," he said.

"Well, hopefully Coldwell won't be able to evict you from there," I said.

"I wouldn't put anything past him," Carter murmured. We both stopped talking when three shiny black cars pulled up out the front of the theater and from each of them four men emerged dressed in black suits, wearing mirrored sunglasses. They were all hulking giants, seemingly printed from the same press. They moved over towards the protesters who were still chanting and walking around with their signs.

"I can't believe they would be so stupid to send hired goons. This is going to go *so* badly," Carter said in breathless anticipation. He started fumbling for his phone, obviously hoping to film an altercation that he could publish online.

The men must have been well trained however. Four of them took up positions at the front of the theater after politely making their way through the protesters, and the rest went inside. The four outside stood there with their hands clasped in front of them wearing their mirrored glasses, standing like statues.

"Why are there guards? Is it about the poisoning?" Carter asked me.

I sighed, folded up the piece of paper and stuffed it in my bag.

"I honestly don't know. I just got here myself. I'll talk to my family and see if there's anything I can find out about Coldwell but honestly I'm not a journalist so there's probably nothing I can do about it," I said.

I saw Peta get out of her car and so I took this opportunity to say goodbye to Carter and rushed across to her so we could make our way through the protesters together. It was only once we got inside that I saw she had a bruise on her cheek.

"What happened, did someone hit you?" I said.

"That's exactly right! Some crazy girl who I think was one of *those* crazy girls who was chasing Jonas walked up to me in the street yesterday and punched me in the face."

"Oh my goddess, are you okay? What happened?"

"I'm okay, I ducked but she still scraped me. It looks a lot worse than it is. I pushed her away and then she ran in her ridiculously high heels down the street. I think those crazy girls need to get the memo that Jonas has a girlfriend now and it's me, so let it go," she said.

We moved away from the door and were halfway down the aisle, so we were out of earshot of the guards near the door and the milling teenagers and actors down near the stage.

I lowered my voice. "Where did this happen?" I said.

"It was down the street, on the corner. I was on my way to the supermarket and it happened out of the blue. Why?" Peta said.

"I don't have the time to tell you right now but there's something magical going on. We'll talk at lunch," I said.

I couldn't help but think of what Aunt Cass had said. Wherever this salamander went it intensified the feelings of love until they became so strong that they turned to jealousy and hatred and violence. Even before the salamander had been in town there had been fights over Jonas when it had spread around town that the young, handsome, real estate developer had been looking for a wife. It had gotten so bad that a fight had broken out between two girls and their mothers outside Jonas's office and when he tried to intervene he had been hit in the head with a full glass tray of brownies, which had knocked him out and sent him to the hospital. I couldn't help but wonder whether the influence of the salamander was causing those girls to go crazy again.

The door swung open as a few more cast members arrived and I felt a jolt of electricity that ran down my spine. There, on the other side of the road, were a couple I'd seen some months ago. It was a woman and a man who'd come to stay at Torrent mansion. The man was wearing the same absurd costume he was back then. He had ridiculously thick glasses, a bright plaid coat, and a Hawaiian T-shirt. His teeth were yellow and oversized. The woman standing beside him had blonde hair, heading to white, stuck up in a pile on her head like a beehive that was so heavy you'd think it might tip over at any moment.

Just like last time she was wearing a blue trench coat over a plaid shirt. She was standing across the road holding a video camera in her hands.

I don't know what it was that made me go crazy, perhaps the protesters, perhaps Mom telling me snitches get stitches, or seeing my friend with a bruise. Whatever it was I rushed back out of the theater, burst through the protesters and crossed the road.

"Hey what are you doing? Why are you filming us?" I called out to the couple.

They both bolted, putting on a surprising turn of speed as they sprinted away from me down the street and around the corner.

For some reason this made me even angrier and I followed, chasing after them. By the time I turned the corner they were down the street getting into an old car with a rental sticker on the window.

It started with a cough and then roared away. It took everything I had in me to not fling some sort of spell at them, something to break the car, to make them stop.

It was only when they turned the corner and disappeared from view that the feeling of anger began to subside and I found myself wondering how I could be so stupid as to think I would cast a spell in full daylight, likely in view of others. Yes, they had been filming the theater but perhaps they'd been filming the protesters. They were certainly weird and had been at the Torrent mansion at some point, but they hadn't done anything to me. Could this be the salamander? How strong was its influence?

I marched back to the theater, past the protesters and the guards, and went inside. The director was already calling everyone in, explaining that the guards were private security who would be roaming the theater to ensure that everyone was kept safe. As I joined the group I couldn't stop myself thinking that we certainly needed a lot more than giant men in mirrored sunglasses to keep us safe from whatever supernatural things were going on in Harlot Bay.

CHAPTER EIGHT

J was so engrossed in Hans's "autobiography" that I didn't realize someone had spoken to me until they reached down and touched me on the shoulder.

I heard a burst of music, piano layered over piano, echoing as though in a concert hall. Solemn low tones and fast jaunty music mixed. It came in a burst of sound and then it was gone. When I looked up I saw it was Marcus Fyfe, the music director, who had touched me.

"Oh, I'm sorry, I didn't see you there. What did you say?" I said.

"I said did you hear? The great director is awake," Marcus said with a smile.

Days had slipped by, as they do. Rehearsal still continued, guards loomed about the place putting a serious kink in the teenagers' plans to kiss and canoodle away in darkened corners. The protesters turned out to be some of the politest protesters I'd ever seen. They stood outside the theater every day protesting and chanting, but let us come and go. They were still staying at the Torrent mansion, which certainly good for the moms and their income, although it meant I hadn't gone down to that end of the mansion because I didn't want to see any of them at all. No one had been injured, nothing else had been sabotaged, and we hadn't captured the salamander yet. It seemed like life had returned to some normality. Aunt Cass had certainly made herself scarce. Every time I went to find her I couldn't, and if I rang she didn't answer her phone. We were quickly approaching the nights when we were to collect water samples to track down the salamander, according to Aunt Cass's list of times, dates and locations.

"Really? He's awake? Is he talking?" I said.

"Apparently he is. He claims he was poisoned, which of course we know he was, and that soon he will return to put on the finest production of the *Taming of the Shrew* the world has ever seen," Marcus said, dramatically waving his arm.

He imitated Hans so well that I laughed and we both rolled our eyes. Yes, part of me was glad that Hans wasn't dead and now was awake and speaking, but at the same time the man was a colossal, gigantic, enormous, huge, and every other word that meant massively big, horrible *pain* who had an ego so large you could hook ropes to it and use it to ferry passengers across the Atlantic.

"Join me?" I asked Marcus.

"Sure," he said and took a seat across from me.

We were in the Pie Barons, which was one of the local pie shops that served an extraordinary range of delicious pies. After three days of rehearsal the director had declared today we'd have a two-hour lunch break. Normally I would have gone to *Traveler* to hang out with my cousins, but since they'd been given the approval to expand into the building next door they'd been hard at work transforming it into a cafe so they could serve food. They had hired a local to knock down part of the wall in between the two buildings to make a thoroughfare, and were busy cleaning and fixing the interior.

The waitress came to our table and took Marcus's order and after she left he tapped his finger on my book.

"Do you love the dear director so much that you're reading his autobiography now?" Marcus asked.

"Oh yes, that's exactly what's happening. He's such a fascinating character and I want to be just like him," I said, deadpan. "I was just reading it because I thought maybe it could give me a clue as to if there was anyone who hated him enough to poison him. But that list has a lot of people on it," I said.

"I think most of the theater community he's ever worked with could certainly be called in for questioning," Marcus agreed.

I was about halfway through the autobiography and what I'd discovered was that Hans had made enemies everywhere he'd gone since he'd been a child. He'd quite modestly put this down to his *genius*, but even though the autobiography would surely have been written in his favor it was easy to read between the lines, especially now that I knew him personally. His arrogant ways caused him to make enemies and those enemies often did things to him, including one of them stabbing him. He'd been stabbed, had a bottle of wine smashed on his head, been shoved off a stage into an orchestra pit, and even at one point claimed to have a bounty on his head. His autobiography was a mixture of stories of disaster like this, and triumphs as he'd began to put on Shakespeare performances that were successful. In every scene and chapter, he was portrayed as the hero. There was an entire chapter devoted to his early twenties when he claimed he'd worked with a director who had failed to take care of safety on set and as a result, there had been an explosion and a fire in which six actors had died as well as three of the audience. After ripping the director to pieces, Hans had written that this event had given him a special appreciation for life and he was going to seize it and never give up doing what he was put on this earth to do.

I had rolled my eyes many times during that chapter, noticing that he had completely forgotten that people had died in that incident, but somehow he brought the story right back around to him as the center of it.

Marcus's pie and drink arrived and he started eating. I'd already eaten mine and I had been reading, trying to find anything or anyone who might be a suspect.

"Does it list his ex-wives in there? If anyone were going to poison him it would definitely be one of them," Marcus said through a mouthful of pie.

"I haven't got to that part yet, but I'm sure it does and I'm sure he was the hero and they were the ones who couldn't appreciate his so-called genius," I said.

We started chatting away about the play. Marcus had worked with Hans for the last two years as musical director, saying the same thing many did who worked with Hans: they did it because it was good for their career.

"But I think this might be the last time on the merry-go-round. Having sandbags land on the stage and a director poisoned ain't good," Marcus said.

I glanced out the front window and saw a familiar figure across the road. It was Henry G, costume designer. With him was Olivia, one of the other assistants on the play. They were walking down the street, Henry G waving his arms around and talking as he always did and Olivia gazing at him with puppy dog eyes. Marcus looked back over his shoulder at them and then turned back to me, raising his eyebrows as he did.

"That poor girl needs to understand that she is not his type," Marcus said.

"Does she like him?" I said.

"Have you seen the way she looks at him? She is in love

but I don't think she knows that Henry G would only be interested if her name was *Oliver* and not Olivia," Marcus said.

That familiar feeling returned, the one of slight anxiety mixed with intuition.

"How long has that been going on?" I asked

"I think maybe since we arrived in Harlot Bay? It's fairly recent," Marcus said.

I sighed and tried to take my mind off it but I just couldn't get away from the thought that Olivia's love wasn't real and was perhaps being influenced by supernatural means.

Love potions are certainly nothing new to a witch and at various times we had experimented with them. Most witches quickly learn the truth: fake love is not as good as real love. The thing was that sometimes fake love became real love over time. Ethics aside, we try to avoid using love potions although the moms had dabbled, at times dosing food for boys that they thought we should date.

It seemed this salamander had the same effect, causing love where love shouldn't be and heartbreak was sure to follow.

"I'm sure she'll work it out and then she'll get over it," Marcus said.

"Yeah, I hope so," I said.

"So who's on your list of suspects?" Marcus said.

"Well, I have the new director because he obviously benefits from taking over; virtually everyone who worked with Hans, including myself, who benefit from not having to be around Hans; and then of course there's every single person in the history of time who's ever encountered him who benefits by getting their revenge. So it's a fairly short list and I'm going to crack this case wide open fairly soon," I said.

He finished his lunch and it was time for us to return to the theater. We walked back, passed by the protesters and went inside, Marcus heading back to the piano. I went out to the dressing rooms to see if any of the teenagers were around and found one of the doors closed. I grabbed it and pulled it open, expecting to find a smooching couple on the other side, but I only found Fox, one of the boys in the play. He was sitting in a chair, crying softly to himself, his eyes red.

There had been a bit of this going on and although I could attribute some of it to the salamander the rest was just teenagers being teenagers.

I closed the door behind me, pulled up a chair and sat in front of him.

"So what happened? Is it Amaris?" I asked.

Fox nodded and tried to wipe away his tears but more kept coming.

"I stole her something but she doesn't like it," he said.

Oh boy, I thought. Was this how the moms had felt dealing with us? What I wanted to say was "What are you doing stealing things? Don't you realize how absurd it is to steal something just because someone tells you that? And by the way, if someone tests you like that for love, you don't want that love because it's not love at all!" I didn't say any of this of course because I knew he would immediately shut down.

"Just try to focus on the play and soon it'll be over and you'll find someone else, believe me," I said.

This probably wasn't the best thing to say either because it started a fresh burst of tears but then he quickly wiped them away and left the room. I was sitting there sighing to myself when a soft form brushed past my legs.

"Two people in costumes up at the mansion snooping around," Adams said.

"Did one of them have crazy blonde hair and was wearing a plaid shirt?" I asked, sitting bolt upright.

"I don't know, I wasn't paying attention. I was sleeping

and they woke me up but now they're snooping and I want to sleep," Adams said.

He stepped between my legs and then when I looked under my chair he was gone.

I quickly rang Mom but her phone went to voicemail. Either she was still busy at the house or she'd gone off to the bakery. Molly and Luce were hard at work and Aunt Ro and Aunt Freya were at the bakery too. I didn't want to call the police so I rang Jack instead.

"Adams just told me two people are snooping around Torrent mansion, do you think you can check it out?" I said.

"Did he get a description?" Jack asked, his voice serious.

"He's a cat so his description was two people but I think I saw them across from the theater filming the protesters, and I saw them at the Mansion a couple of months ago. They stayed there. For some reason they were wearing disguises," I said.

"Okay, I'll get out there right now and see what I can find. I'll let you know," Jack said. The phone went dead, leaving me in the silence of the dressing room.

"Does anything else want to happen?" I asked the wall, throwing my hands up in the air.

The wall didn't answer but the piercing scream from the main part of the theater certainly did.

CHAPTER NINE

"I think you should just quit," Molly said, picking a piece of fluff off her black balaclava.

"What kind of snake do they think it is?" Luce asked.

"They don't know officially but of course in all the chaos the teenagers still took photos with their phones and then looked it up on the Internet. It has stripes and matches exactly an Australian tiger snake," I said. I adjusted my black top and then quickly checked myself in the mirror.

"Director gets poisoned, sandbags falling and even with all the guards there, there's still a snake let loose? Sounds like an inside job to me," Molly said.

"Yeah, maybe you're right," I said. I walked over to the kitchen table where Aunt Cass's map of the storm drains was laid out. Tonight was the first night we were to go out to collect water samples. It was just past ten and I'd much rather be sleeping. My cousins, for some reason, seemed strangely eager to get down into the stormwater system although I had no idea why.

"We need to make this fast because I am super tired," I complained.

It had been an extraordinarily long day. After the snake had appeared in the theater the police had been called and then an animal control officer who'd captured the snake. Then there had been more questioning, everyone talking to the police again and this time they wouldn't let anyone leave until they had spoken to every single person in the theater, including all the private security. We'd essentially sat around for hours while the police interrogated everyone to see if they had any information as to where the snake might've come from.

As far as I knew no one had cracked under questioning and admitted it was them. Thankfully no one had been bitten. The snake was more scared of us than we were of it, although you wouldn't have thought so according to the screams. I briefly talked to Sheriff Hardy who had told me he was on the brink of shutting the whole play down in the interest of public safety. The director declared the show must go on which reminded me of the note that had been found beside Hans. Thus far the police couldn't shut us down although it was fairly clear there was someone working with malicious intent.

I told Jack about it and he too had echoed Molly's sentiments. I should stop working on the play. Between people snooping around the mansion (Jack hadn't found them) and everything else going on, continuing to work on the play wasn't the safe move. I'd mentioned this to Kira, who had flatly refused to give up her position as Katherine. The fact was many of the other teenagers, although scared, felt the same way. Something bad was going on but it wasn't going to stop them from putting on this performance they had rehearsed so long and hard for. For my part, although yes, I did need the money and I was a bit scared, I felt protective over Kira and the other teenagers. Lingering in the back of my mind was what Aunt Cass had said to me: there's something strange in Harlot Bay. I had no real idea if this was connected to it or just one of those things that happened, perhaps exacerbated by the magical confluence that circled above the bay, but I guess at some point I decided that I would be involved and that meant I would stay working for the play, trying to uncover who had poisoned Hans, cut sandbags, and now apparently released a snake into the theater.

Molly went to her bedroom and then returned with a small crowbar in her hands.

"Oh, excellent, is that Aunt Cass's crowbar?" Luce asked.

"No, it's the *family* crowbar. Why does everyone keep saying that?" Molly said, exasperated.

"Big talk from someone who is sure to get cursed one of these days," I said.

"Pish and posh. She's not going to do anything. I think she respects me more now," Molly said. Since the dinner where all the boyfriends had been revealed, including Aunt Cass's Art, Molly had been riding high on finally getting some sort of revenge on Aunt Cass, although it hadn't *entirely* been revenge. Personally I think she was risking getting cursed, but there was a little truth to what she said. Aunt Cass did kind of respect those people who talked back and so for all we knew maybe she wasn't going to do anything to Molly in revenge for the revenge for the revenge.

We grabbed the map, the small glass vials and the extendable grasping claw that Aunt Cass had given us, and then drove Molly's car down the hill.

"This is going be exciting," Molly said, drumming her fingers on the steering wheel.

"What is going on with you two? We're going down into the stormwater drains, which by the way are icky and gross and the two of you seem really happy about it," I said suspiciously.

"Nothing is going on. We're just happy to be helping to solve this mystery to find that salamander," Molly said.

"Poor little thing, it's probably scared out of its wits," Luce said.

"You do realize the poor little thing is making love more intense and then it's going to turn to hatred and people might kill each other because of this salamander," I said.

"It's not its fault. It probably got lost away from its native habitat," Luce said. We drove into town but instead of heading for the manhole cover near where we were to take our first sample, we drove to *Traveler* instead.

"What are we doing here?" I asked as we got out of the car.

"We have to pick up Kira," Molly said.

"Kira is involved?" I asked. Molly unlocked *Traveler*, flicked the lights on and we went inside. I put the map down on the table and sat down, only for Kira to shimmer out of nowhere and shout "Rar!" The three of us squealed and Kira broke out into a cackling witch laughter.

"Ha! Got you all," she said, pointing her fingers at us.

"You better watch it Stern. I could've hit you with a fireball," I said, although I laughed myself.

"Go right ahead. I like fireballs," Kira said. "So, are we ready for some Torrent witch shenanigans? The next exciting chapter in the Torrent and Stern adventures?"

"You want to come down into the stormwater system as well? You do know it's gross down there, right?" I asked.

"Nah I don't want to but my grandma said I had to help you guys to find that salamander, that it is apparently quote 'good for my magical education' unquote, " Kira said.

"So Hattie knows about the salamander too? Is there some secret witch network operating?" I asked.

"Witch internet maybe," Kira quipped.

"Okay, now that we're here, it's time to tell you that we're not just going to be collecting water samples tonight," Molly began.

"Ha! I knew you two were up to something. What is it?" I said.

Luce went out to the back room and then returned with a bag from the *Magic Bean*. From inside she pulled out half a sandwich and then one of Aunt Cass's testing strips which was a deep pink heading towards red.

"We went back and bought another sandwich for forensic analysis," Luce said.

"And do you know what we found? Magic." Molly said.

Luce handed me the testing strip.

"What do you mean you found magic? What did you test with this?" I asked.

"We tested the sandwich. We put the testing strip inside of it and it turned bright pink. They're putting magic in the sandwich and they're beating us and we're going to close down and go broke and become homeless and lead terrible lives unless we do something about it!" Luce said, going slightly off the deep end.

"Oh no, you're about to propose that we break in aren't you?" I asked.

"Come on, it's just a bit of light snooping and mild crime. We saw on the stormwater map there just happens to be a manhole that opens into the small private courtyard behind their shop. We figured we'd collect some samples and then maybe come up there and have a quick look, that's all," Molly said.

"O yeah, Torrent and Stern on a breaking and entering adventure," Kira said, a slightly wild look in her eyes.

"No, this is a terrible idea. What does it matter if they have magic in their sandwiches? We don't have any reason to break into their shop just to discover that," I said.

"Well, we're the witches of Harlot Bay and it's up to us to ensure peace and harmony and that magic is being used responsibly," Molly said primly, as though butter wouldn't melt in her mouth.

"Yeah, plus we really are gonna be in trouble if they keep selling magic sandwiches and we don't get any business," Luce added.

"I don't know, this doesn't sound good," I said.

Kira tapped her nails on the map. "I know you're hesitant Harlow, but they're right. People dosing sandwiches with magic? That's going into food that people are eating. Who knows what that could do? At the very least it's a public health violation. At the worst who knows, maybe people are going to grow a third eye or something. As the witches of this town we need to have a look into this," Kira said, sounding like a reasonable grown-up proposing a reasonable plan.

"Okay, three against one, I'll help you," I sighed.

We went quickly over the plan. We were going to grab some water samples where we were meant to, but then we'd take a detour, go up through the manhole cover into the small private courtyard behind the *Magic Bean*, then we'd use a magic unlocking spell to go inside to investigate. It sounded simple but then most of our plans sounded simple and most our plans came to some disaster of one kind or another.

"Okay, let's go," Molly said.

We left *Traveler*, turning the lights off and locking it up. We got back in the car and drove a few streets away (mostly because all four of us were completely dressed in black and probably looked highly suspicious lurking around the streets). Down a small side street we found the manhole cover that was our entry into the stormwater drains. Molly used the family crowbar to open it up and then we all slipped inside, pulling the manhole cover back into place above us. When we were underground Kira and Luce each summoned a light which lit up the stormwater drains. They pretty much looked like the drains where Jack and I had gone. They were grimy, wet, there was flowing water, and it didn't smell very good.

We walked along until we found the junction where Aunt Cass had indicated on our map we were to take a sample. There was a slight bit of argument at that point because the water level was quite a bit lower than we'd expected and someone had to lay on the ground to get the sample, even with the extendable arm. Molly lost that argument, and eventually lay down, extended the arm and collected the water which she quickly dipped the test strip into and then put it into a small case that Aunt Cass had given us. We continued on our way until we reached another junction and this time it was my turn to lay down, get covered in grime and whatever else was on the ground, to collect some water. We still had another sample to collect but now it was time for the detour. We took a junction and walked about two streets underground until we came to a rusting ladder with a small manhole at the top. Molly went first, using the crowbar to lever the manhole up and then creeping out.

"It's clear," she whispered down the hole. Luce, Kira and I followed, Luce and Kira extinguishing the floating lights so we were plunged into darkness. We emerged into a small private courtyard behind the *Magic Bean*. There was nothing much there, just some scrubby grass, a few cobblestones, and the manhole cover. The area was too small for them to do anything with and so it essentially sat there neglected. Because we were overshadowed by the buildings and there were no streetlights nearby, the whole area was in the dark and lit only by the slight amount of moonlight.

"Come on, let's go," Kira urged, her eyes gleaming in the dark.

We crept up to the back door which was two doors: a heavy mesh security and then a wooden door behind it. Kira went first, casting an unlocking spell to take out the mesh door, and then when she yawned at the effort, Luce took over, unlocking the next door. We'd all slipped our balaclavas on, an act that felt incredibly criminal, and then Molly opened the door and we crept inside.

The *Magic Bean*, like many shops in Harlot Bay, had thick blinds that they pulled down at the end of each day to cover their windows. Even so, we couldn't risk turning on the lights because it would be obvious that someone was inside. So we summoned up small lights instead, letting them drift in front of us, careful not to make them too bright. The back door of *Magic Bean* entered into a large kitchen space with gleaming shelves, stoves and other cookware. We spread out, careful not to touch anything. On some of the surfaces there were piles of metal bowls stacked up that would make an almighty racket if they were knocked over.

"This way, it's their walk-in cool room," Luce whispered. We crept our way to the cool room, opened the door and went inside.

It was stocked to the rafters with all different kinds of produce: salamis, cheeses, olives in jars and the like. There were vegetables, fresh lettuces, tomatoes and some packages of bread as well. Molly and Luce quickly found jars of mayonnaise, one of which Luce said felt highly suspicious. She opened the lid and Molly dipped a test strip in. It immediately turned pink.

"So they're using magic mayonnaise?" I whispered.

"Oh it is so delicious you wouldn't believe it and quite nice to eat while watching their very scruffy and handsome guitarist," Kira said.

"Traitor," Luce muttered.

"We should take this with us," Molly said.

"What for? We already know that there's magic in it. We need to find the source, like what are they mixing into the mayonnaise or where does it come from?" I said.

Luce resealed the mayonnaise and then turned the jar over. On the bottom it had "Made in France" and an address.

"I think this is just ordinary mayonnaise that's coming from France and then someone's putting something magic in it," I said.

"Um guys? If there was an alarm would that be like a red flashing light?" Kira asked.

I was already tense enough but when she said that it felt like every muscle stiffened in an instant. Kira let her light drift up to the corner which revealed the black box with a small red flashing light on it.

"I think that's a silent alarm, we gotta go," Luce said.

She took a step, Molly accidently jostled her, and then there was an enormous crack and splatter as the jar of mayonnaise hit the ground and broke into a million pieces.

"Oh goddess we're dead," I groaned. Kira took the lead, bolting out of the cool room and back through the kitchen and out the back door. As we went out we could hear voices of two men talking out in the alleyway just behind the back fence. They had flashlights, the light gleaming up the brick wall of the buildings around us.

We were in a frantic rush. Molly left the manhole cover off, but she had to go down last so she could pull it in place with the crowbar. Kira went first, followed by me then Luce and then Molly next. She'd just managed to pull the manhole cover into place when the back gate opened up and we heard the men go through. We all waited there in the dark, panting. We could hear every word they were saying.

"The back door's open. Maybe they're still inside," one of the men said.

"I'll have a look around," the other one said.

"We have to get out of here," I whispered.

No one had to be told twice. We went down the ladder, summoned lights and went racing through the stormwater drains as fast as we could, just short of running. No one wanted to fall off an edge into the water. Soon we were back at the manhole cover where we had entered but as we were climbing Kira whispered "What if the police are driving around? They're going to see us for sure. We're all dressed in black. We look like criminals."

Molly stopped on the ladder and sighed.

"Okay, we do a concealment spell, get out of here, back to my car, and if we all work together maybe we can get back to the mansion without getting caught," she said.

"That sounds awesome and all but as you may remember I'm a Slip witch and I'm not doing so well on concealment spells right now," Kira said.

"How are you doing, Harlow?" Molly asked.

"I don't know, I feel okay. It's one of those things you don't know how bad it's going to go until you do it."

"Well, we can't stay down here forever, we have to leave! Who knows, maybe they'll send someone down to the stormwater drains and then we'll get caught," Luce said.

With that, Molly used the crowbar to pry open the manhole cover and then peeked out. There was no one in sight but she still cast a concealment spell over the hole and then quickly crept out. We followed, pulling the manhole closed. Molly was fine until all four of us were out of the hole and she suddenly passed out and collapsed on the ground.

Her concealment spell flickered out.

"Hey!" a male voice shouted in the distance.

"Oh crap," I yelped. Without thinking I pulled on the magic around me and cast a concealment spell. I may have gone a *little* too far. The magic around me roared, and the four of us disappeared. I mean that literally. When I held out my hand in front of my face I couldn't see it.

"Holy moly, Torrent," Kira said.

"Just stand still, be quiet," Luce said. We saw a man approaching. He was wearing a private security outfit and carrying a torch. He walked up to where we were standing and then walked by, unable to see us. We stood there holding our breaths, hoping he wouldn't bump into any of us. He soon turned the corner.

"Okay, let's grab Molly and get home," Luce said.

That was a debacle of the highest order. It took a lot of shuffling around to find Molly, us bumping into each other until we could finally pick her up and carry her out of the small side street and back to the car.

"Is this spell pulling on you? Are you going to be okay?" Luce asked.

"I can't feel a thing, it's like it's taking no energy at all," I whispered back.

Molly had the keys which we discovered when we tried to find them and they dropped onto the ground, and then we spent five minutes searching for an invisible jangling set of keys. Finally we found them, unlocked the car and got inside, only to be presented with our final problem. Although it was close to eleven, there was still traffic around Harlot Bay, including some cars driving around that we were sure were private security that had been summoned by the silent alarm. I tentatively tried to cast a concealment spell to cover the car but nothing worked. There was no response from the magic. Whatever spell I'd cast was too powerful and was dominating everything. We are invisible and we'd have to drive the car out of Harlot Bay that way.

"Let's just do it. People will ignore it or they'll glance and think it's a little old grandma who's so small she can't even see over the steering wheel," Luce said. She started the car and drove as fast as possible out of Harlot Bay. We passed at least three cars and every driver looked into ours with amazed expressions, puzzled as to where our driver was. We finally made it out of Harlot Bay and headed back up the hill. We reached the mansion and drove down to our end where we quickly leaped out of the car and ran inside, dragging the unconscious Molly with us, to find Adams on the sofa watching a documentary about sea lions.

"I'm hungry. Did you bring any cheese?" Adams asked me.

"Can you see us?" I asked.

He glanced away from the television and then back again. "Nope, I could smell you though. Have you been underground?"

"Oh, my head," Molly groaned from the chair we'd dropped her in. The freakout started a few seconds later.

"I'm invisible? Harlow, I'm invisible, I can't go to work if I'm invisible!" she said.

"Do you think *I* can?"

"Well undo it, let it go. We're finished, we're safe home," she said.

I sat down the sofa, closed my eyes and took a breath, trying to feel the magic around me, searching for the spell but I couldn't find it.

"This is super cool being invisible but yeah, I need to be *visible* if I'm going to be in the play. I am one of the stars," Kira commented.

"It's not working, I can't feel it. I don't know what's happening," I said desperately.

"Let's wait. Maybe it'll wear off by itself," Luce said.

She made us four cups of coffee, decaf in deference to the late hour, which we all had to fetch off the bench individually because we couldn't see each other for her to deliver them to us. We all sat in sort of a stunned silence, drinking our coffee (which by the way didn't magically appear in our stomach drifting there in space; it was invisible too) and watching the documentary on sea lions with Adams. Midnight came and went. Kira fell asleep on the sofa, or so we thought given we could hear slight snoring, and then, just as it hit one o'clock we all reappeared, the spell wearing off with a popping noise like a bubble breaking.

I was bleary eyed but intensely relieved. Luce shook Kira awake.

"Hey Stern, you're visible again. Come on, I'll give you a lift home," she said.

"Keep it real Torrents, it's been fun," Kira said sleepily and followed Luce out to the car.

"I need to go to bed. That was a disaster. We shouldn't do anything like that again," I said to Molly.

Molly looked down at her black pants, which had been splattered with mayonnaise.

"It wasn't a *complete* disaster. We have proof they're putting magic in food which I'm going to tell Aunt Cass once we've thought about things a little more and I'm sure she's going to be able to do something about it. I know coincidentally it might help out *Traveler* but really, magic in food? It can't be safe," Molly said.

I said goodnight and went off to bed, taking off my pants that were doused in mayonnaise too and rolled them up so Adams wouldn't be tempted to lick them clean. He soon followed me and curled up at the end my bed as I lay there in the dark, feeling intensely tired but somehow unable to sleep. All I had tried to do was cast a concealment spell and yet I had made the four of us completely invisible, even to ourselves, and then had no way to undo it. What if it had been something else? What if when Kira had leaped out to scare us I'd cast a fireball in fear? I could have incinerated her on the spot or burned *Traveler* to the ground. It was an unsettling feeling that stuck with me until I finally drifted off to sleep for a night of restless dreams.

CHAPTER TEN

"*T*hese fifteen years! By my fay, a goodly nap. But did I never speak of all that time?" Aunt Cass said in her costume of Christopher Sly.

"Yes, yes! Perfection. That's exactly what I want," Emilion said, shouting out loud and clapping his hands.

I watched from a distance and groaned to myself. I certainly had enough on my plate and things were chaotic enough without Aunt Cass getting involved in the play but here she was having apparently auditioned successfully to play the role of Christopher Sly, the drunken Tinker.

"You have it, you're perfect. I don't need to see any more," Emilion said.

I have to admit that Henry G had done an incredible job of making up Aunt Cass. She did in fact look like a man who had lived rough for many years. Her nose was red from too much drinking and she looked to be in her forties with a light stubble and bedraggled hair.

It had been quite an incredible transformation and one in fact that I'd been unaware was going to happen until I arrived at the theater and found Aunt Cass in makeup with

Henry G affixing her new eyebrows. With everyone around I couldn't unload on her as to why exactly she was in the play. When Christopher had dropped out after being hit with a sandbag, the director said that they would find someone else and for some reason Aunt Cass had taken it upon herself to fill the position. As I watched, Aunt Cass stood up on the stage and took a bow and then went off, her audition over, so Emilion could continue rehearsing the rest of the play.

I sat back in my chair and let out a sigh. I hadn't caught up on last night's lost sleep whatsoever, being forced out of bed in the early morning by Adams meowing and scratching at the door like a lunatic. For a cat who could appear and disappear anywhere he wanted, there were times he simply reverted to pretending he was a cat who needed every door opened for him by hand. After that I couldn't get back to sleep, the anxiety of last night returning. I had faced my two exhausted cousins in the morning, who were both a little shell-shocked that we'd been pursued and almost caught the previous night but at the same time they were both happy that they'd discovered the mayonnaise and had collected samples on their clothing. For my part, I was worried that we'd get caught. It seemed obvious if someone had broken into the *Magic Bean* wouldn't it be a good guess that the culprits were the only other coffee shop in town who was their direct rival?

Molly and Luce had both dismissed this, a little too quickly for my liking, appearing to think that if they didn't say it out loud then it couldn't possibly come true.

I yawned, unable to help myself, as teenagers came on and began rehearsing another scene. It was going to be another ridiculously long day. Today was a slightly early finish from the play but then I had to work at the library, which meant I wouldn't be finishing until a least eight. Although I would be sitting and sorting papers, I know what

I'd much rather be doing: eating food at Jack's and then sleeping for a hundred years.

Thinking of Jack, I realized I hadn't told him what had happened last night. This was not one of those conversations you have over the phone where you admit to crimes. I'd have to tell him in person but I still wasn't seeing him until at least maybe tomorrow or on the weekend.

As I sat there watching the rehearsal, my mind drifted. I realized there were quite a few things I just simply didn't have the time for. I hadn't been back to my lair in some days, I hadn't written anything on my story, I hadn't seen John Smith except for that time he'd jumped off the three-story building in town. My poor office was sitting vacant and abandoned. I don't think I'd been back there for at least two or three weeks now. Under the rules of the free rent program you had to use your office at least three days out of five or risk losing it, given that one of the key points was to make sure the buildings were occupied to stop vandalism and to encourage other businesses to start. I knew I was breaking the rules but I simply didn't have the time to go back to my office, nor any real reason to. I'm sure if I returned there I would likely find a pile of twenty dollar bills sitting on the desk from John Smith, who still arrived for therapy sessions. That was just something else to feel guilty about but it was a small pain only. I hadn't been able to help him, not at all, and even though Ollie had given me a list of names and newspaper articles of acapella groups, I hadn't been able to find anything in them that would lead me to discover who John Smith had been in his life. The sad thing was that John was under the delusion that he wasn't a ghost, that he wasn't dead. That had been something he'd shouted at me the last time he remembered something from his past.

Speaking of things I was letting slide by, I hadn't talked to the moms or the rest of the family about Coldwell and the mall either. Carter had requested that I do but with everything happening there just seemed to be no point to it. The moms were busy with the bakery and now Aunt Ro and Sheriff Hardy's upcoming wedding. The protesters were still in residence and I'd been avoiding going down there and so I'd barely seen my mom and aunts either. I sometimes felt like I was back in high school and hadn't done any of my homework from multiple classes and now it was piling up to such a degree that I was paralyzed, unable to move on any of it. That included talking with Hattie Stern about the fact that her ancestor's journal had shown me the past and then given me a weapon to defeat the Shadow Witch. I hadn't spoken to Hattie about it, hadn't told her what I'd seen, I guess perhaps relying on the idea that she and Aunt Cass, although apparently mortal enemies, seemed to communicate with each other.

The rehearsal dragged on as I watched and eventually I was called to help with costume changes. Time thankfully slipped by and soon it was the late afternoon and soon we were finished. The theater was locked up and we left, all the teenagers babbling excitedly, ignoring the protesters who were still being quite polite but getting increasingly noisy, shouting out their slogans at us. Not much had come of the protest. Carter had covered it in his paper, of course, but because there had been no fights and there was no footage of anyone getting dragged away, there wasn't much more to report on the story. Not to say that Carter hadn't tried. He had of course interviewed the leader, Galina, describing her opposition to the *Taming of the Shrew* being performed.

I was marching back to my car so tired and glazed over that I didn't see Sheriff Hardy until I bumped into him.

"Oh Sheriff, sorry," I said and gave an enormous yawn.

"Were you out late last night?" Sheriff Hardy said, his face impassive.

111

There was no tone in his voice, nothing threatening or scary, but I felt like I'd had a bucket of ice water thrown on me. He hadn't asked me if I'd been up late last night or had slept badly. No, he had asked me *had I been out late last night.* He *knew.* He absolutely knew it was me and probably my cousins. I quickly scrambled for a lie.

"Nope, just working long hours with the rehearsals and also at the library, which is where I'm going right now actually, I really can't stop to chat," I said, trying to step around him. He moved across to block my way and touched me on the arm. In my tired state, I felt the slip magic tingle. I heard the Sheriff's voice talking in low tones about police matters, but then over the top of it came the sound of a wedding march played by a violin.

What was that? Was I hearing things from the future now? Or had Sheriff Hardy been married in the past?

"Persons unknown broke into the *Magic Bean* coffee shop last night," Sheriff Hardy said.

"Oh wow, that's terrible. Did they steal anything?" I said.

"Just some property damage, a jar of mayonnaise I believe smashed on the ground. One of the suspects left some footprints in it actually," he said.

That feeling of being doused with a bucket of ice water hit me again, and my tiredness fled. I resisted the urge to look down at my shoes, which were, in fact, the same shoes I'd been wearing last night. I'd wiped the mayonnaise off them in the morning.

"Well good luck, I hope you catch them," I said for some crazy reason. Sheriff Hardy gave me a level look.

"Well nothing was stolen, so I think this is going to be one of those cases that probably goes unsolved. I just hope that those involved aren't stupid enough to do anything like that again," he said.

"That sounds good," I croaked. Sheriff Hardy stepped

aside and continued his way up the street. I managed to gather myself together and walked back to my car before driving around to the library. By the time I got there, the shock had begun to wear off, and my sleepiness was starting to return. I knew we shouldn't have broken into the *Magic Bean*! Even though we *could* argue it was because we'd discovered there was magic in their food. Given there was now a footprint on the scene it seemed that evidence that would tie one of us to it but it appeared the Sheriff had given us a pass. After all, there had been no witnesses to see or catch us. I understood all too well though what he was saying. Despite the fact he was going to become our relative in a few short days, there was no way he could let crimes like breaking and entering slip by unpunished.

I went into the library saying hello to Constance Osterman who was at the front counter. She was Kaylee's mom. I was still training with Kaylee although it had gone down to maybe once a week now with all the extra jobs I had going on.

"He's downstairs again," Constance said.

"Thanks, have a good night," I said. The library would be closing soon. Given I was working late they'd given me a key so I could let myself out and lock up when I left.

I went downstairs to find Ollie covered in dust sitting cross-legged with piles of paper scattered around him. As I may have mentioned before, my job is essentially taking piles of paper and separating them into new piles. Ollie would then decide out of those which would be digitized. He'd been mostly focusing on family histories and crimes these were the most exciting things in the hope that we could get more funding to digitize the entire collection. He was sitting amongst the piles of paper muttering to himself and looking at them. He picked a piece up and then threw it forcefully down.

"Hey Ollie, you okay?" I asked.

"No, I'm not okay. I think a lot of these documents have been forged but I don't understand how," he said. I put my bag down and then sat on the floor across from him to have a look at the pile of paper he'd been dropping pages onto. The first piece of paper looked like a pay record of some kind, showing how much someone had been paid for building work out on Truer Island.

"Well this looks like a payment record for a builder on Truer Island. Why would you think this is forged?" I asked.

Ollie tugged at his hair and gritted his teeth.

"You're right, they're pay records for a building on Truer Island. It must be a big building because all of *this* pile are pay records as well, and what's the biggest building we have out on Truer Island?" he asked.

"It has to be the Governor's mansion, right?" I said.

"That's what I thought too except *this isn't for the Governor's mansion.* This is something else entirely. It would have to be the size of a mansion out on Truer Island and it doesn't exist on any map," he said.

That bucket of ice came sloshing towards me again. I knew instantly what he was talking about. He was right. There was a mansion out on Truer Island that I suspected wouldn't be on any maps, except one. Molly, Luce and I had followed the birds carved into tree trunks out onto Truer Island to find the creepy mansion, which looked very similar to Torrent mansion.

We'd barely escaped and once we had, we couldn't find the mansion again. I couldn't tell Ollie this however. He didn't know we were witches and what could I say? Yeah, you're right. There is a mansion out there but it's hidden under a spell?

"Did you find anything else?" I asked, hesitantly.

"I found a map that shows buildings that don't exist, there

are dates that don't match up, there are gaps where there should be no gap. How old is Aunt Cass?" he asked

"She's in her eighties," I said, a little unsure myself.

"That's right, she is in her eighties, and she looks like she's in her eighties, and all the paperwork you could ever find about her would pin her to being in her eighties. Can you tell me how old Hattie Stern is?" he asked.

"She looks to be early sixties, I think? I mean she is Kira's grandmother, and she has a daughter, and that daughter had Kira," I said.

"Right, so she's in her early sixties and Aunt Cass is in her eighties and then we have this," he said, handing me a copy of a newspaper article. The title was *Ocean Swimming Trio Win Big!* I couldn't read the story because my eyes had prickled with sudden tears. It was Grandma April, Aunt Cass and Hattie, sixteen years old if they were a day, grinning toothy smiles in black and white at the camera.

"Maybe Hattie just looks young," I said, not believing it myself.

"I don't think that's true, Harlow. I think Hattie is the same age as your Aunt but for some reason she looks like she's sixty. *All* of these pieces of paper here are wrong, dates that are wrong, people who should still be around but have disappeared, gaps everywhere. Harlow, there's something deeply wrong with the world," Ollie said.

I saw his hands were shaking. Without thinking I reached out to touch them. There came a burst of sound and this one wasn't good. It was Molly shouting, pleading, begging and then Ollie shouting back at her. I couldn't understand what they were saying but they were fighting. It was something terrible. It faded away, leaving only an echo of grief behind. Was that the future? Had I just heard Ollie and future Molly breaking up?

"It'll be okay, Ollie," I said, patting him on the hand.

Ollie sighed and looked down at the papers surrounding him.

"I don't see how it can be. I honestly feel like I'm going crazy," he said.

I made an abrupt decision, one that I wish I didn't have to make but there was no lie that could cover this, no little story that would make Ollie feel better. I stood up and then held out my hand to him, which he took and I pulled him up off the ground.

"You need to finish work now and I'm going to as well. Go home, have a shower and then come out to the mansion to see us. I'm going to call Will as well," I said.

"What is this about Harlow? Is something wrong? Is it about Molly?" Ollie asked.

"She'll have to tell you. I'm sorry I can't tell you more. I'm going to go now and I want you to leave too. Please do as I ask and hopefully I'll see you at the mansion very soon," I said. I grabbed my bag and rushed out of there, Ollie following behind me, a look of confusion on his face. He told Constance he was leaving and that she should lock up because I was going too.

I rushed back to my car and then tried to ring Molly and Luce but the diabolical telecommunications of Harlot Bay were not cooperating. I checked the time. With any luck they should be at home by now. Praying to the goddess that my car wouldn't break down I started it up and rushed home, feeling an aching tension running through my body. There was going to be no way around it: Molly and Luce would have to tell their boyfriends that they were witches. Perhaps Luce could have kept the secret from Will a little longer, but it felt cruel, exclusionary. I kept testing my phone on the way home but it refused to cooperate.

When I burst into the house I found Molly and Luce pacing anxiously.

"What's going on, Harlow? Ollie called me and said you told him to come out here and that I've got something to tell him?" Molly said.

"Will's coming too. What is this?" Luce asked.

I sat down at the kitchen table, feeling that I might be sick.

"Ollie knows something is wrong. He found all these papers, dates are wrong, Hattie Stern's age is wrong. I think he even found the building records for that mansion out on Truer Island. He was going crazy like he was getting depressed from it. I think you have to tell him. You have to tell him that you're a witch and you have to tell Will as well, Luce," I said, staring at the table.

I expected perhaps some shrieking or maybe yelling but what I hadn't expected was complete dead silence. Molly flopped down on the sofa and then Luce sat down on the other chair and began biting her nails. The silence stretched out until I could no longer bear it.

"Look, Jack had to find out when he saw me throw a *fireball*. At least you can just tell them and maybe it'll be okay," I said.

"It's not your fault, Harlow. I know it's not," Molly said softly.

"We may as well get it over and done with, see what happens," Luce said.

I knew it wasn't necessarily the *telling* of the secret that was the problem. It was what might happen next. Our own fathers had had us and then left our mothers, refusing to have anything more to do with the family, something we'd put down to the fact that our moms were witches.

It had been something we'd discussed on and off between the three of us and it was a common problem amongst witches generally that holding on to love was difficult. We were secretive by nature and that didn't always work well in a relationship. We had no time to dwell on that though. There came the sound of two cars driving up. Ollie was in one and Will was in the other, his truck with Truer Landscaping emblazoned on the side. Ollie had gone home and cleaned himself up, but Will had come straight from working late and was still looking quite dirty with bits of grass stuck on him. I opened the door and let them in, both men looking extremely worried.

"What's going on Luce, are you okay?" Will asked, rushing over to embrace her.

"What is it?" Ollie asked and did the same.

They didn't answer but instead both of them burst into tears, and I quickly found myself crying too. The poor boys couldn't have been more confused than if a pink elephant had just walked into the room and asked for a sandwich.

"Shh, it's okay, just tell us what's going on, what's the matter?" Will asked.

"We have something we need to tell you," Luce said haltingly. She didn't get to finish that sentence though. There was another interruption in the form of a car roaring up the driveway and skidding to a stop outside, but not quick enough to avoid ramming into the back of Ollie's car, pushing it forward to crunch into the front of the mansion.

"What the hell?" Will asked. We saw two figures jump out of the car and recognized them immediately as Tess and John Donaldson, the owners of the *Magic Bean*. Tess had a baseball bat. John was shouting at her, trying to stop her, just like last time, but she wasn't listening. She kicked the front door open and came screaming into the house.

"You broke into my shop. I know it was you!" she said. She hefted the baseball bat, getting ready to attack the nearest person, which was Molly. Ollie and Will were rushing towards her to stop her when there came a surge of magic, a flash of golden light that hit Tess and John and knocked them flat on their backs. Bits of the light bounced off, breaking into golden flakes that glittered down, showering over the boys. They turned towards Molly and Luce and me who were all standing there with our hands out, glimmering gold still trickling from our fingertips.

"We're witches," Luce said.

"We're magic," Molly added. The boys both looked down at the unconscious Tess and John and the fading glimmers of gold, and then back at the three of us. I lifted my hand and summoned a golden butterfly into being and drifted it across the room.

"We really are," I said, the golden butterfly drifting down to the floor before dissolving.

CHAPTER ELEVEN

"*T*his is madness. I have to call Peta," I gasped to Molly.

"Okay," she said, gulping down the glass of water and leaning back against the wall of the cool room.

I dialed Peta and she picked up straight away. "We need you at *Traveler Cafe* right now, we're getting killed here," I said.

"See you in five," Peta said proving once again why she was an amazing best friend. No questions, no queries, just agreement.

"She'll be here soon," I said to Molly. We each took a deep breath, both of us looking incredibly sweaty and hot and bothered. We were hardly even halfway through the lunch rush and things had collapsed into chaos. Although we were easily twenty or thirty orders behind, there was just no way we could keep going at the pace we had been all morning. And so I asked yet again the question I had asked multiple times already today.

"So you think Ollie's okay?"

Molly smiled at me. She knew I was just asking because I

wanted to be reassured again. "Yes, really, he's okay, he's better than okay. I mean, you know how he is with research, he's just fascinated. He just wants to know more and more. I think we just made all of his research dreams come true maybe," Molly said and gave a little laugh.

"I wish Luce would tell us what happened," I said.

Last night had gone two very different ways for my cousins. After we'd knocked out John and Tess Donaldson from *Magic Bean*, Molly and Luce had taken Ollie and Will up into the forest and gone into separate directions to have some private time to talk with them, leaving me with the unconscious assailants. I had immediately hidden the baseball bat and called Sheriff Hardy who had arrived just as both were waking up from their magically induced stupor. They were both confused about exactly what had happened which Sheriff Hardy covered over by saying that they'd just crashed into the back of Ollie's car and were possibly suffering some shock from the car accident. The damage to the back of Ollie's car wasn't that severe (nor the damage to the front of the mansion), so the reason didn't hold water, and Tess had started trying to argue again, saying that we had obviously broken into the *Magic Bean* for some nefarious purpose. Sheriff Hardy had told her that they were still investigating, but in any case there was no reason for the two of them to ever come back to Torrent mansion and especially not with a baseball bat. He also told them that if he heard of them returning for any reason he would immediately arrest them. John and Tess had driven down the hill with Sheriff Hardy closely following behind them. It wasn't long after that before a stony-faced Will came walking back from the forest with Luce following close behind him, her eyes red from crying. He got in his truck and left without saying a word. Luce rushed inside, ran by me and vanished into her room. I knocked on her door but she wouldn't answer. About half an hour later Molly and Ollie came walking down from the forest hand-in-hand, their fingers entwined, beaming at each other, the very epitome of a couple in love. I'd had to give Molly a secret sign that it hadn't gone well for Luce, and thankfully she managed to understand without us having to say anything out loud. She'd gone with Ollie to his house and said she'd see me the next day at work.

In the morning we'd gotten up and Luce had refused to speak, retreating to only grunts as we'd gotten ready for the day. Telling Will and Ollie that we were all witches couldn't have come at a worse time. It was Saturday and the soft opening of the *Traveler Cafe*. There was no grand opening, not even any advertising. My cousins were just going to open the café and see how it went. I had been roped into work with Molly and Isabella, one of their *Traveler* staff. Luce was going to work on the *Traveler* side of the business making coffees along with Julie.

Given that there had been so few people in the past week coming to *Traveler*, we'd expected maybe only a few customers but had been quite surprised to find there was a continuous flow of people looking for food and coffee. It was only at eleven when Kira came by that we'd discovered the *Magic Bean* had been shut that day, so they could, in Kira's words, "beef up the security to stop people breaking in and stealing their mayonnaise."

It seemed that every customer of *Magic Bean* had been diverted to our cafe, many of them by Kira herself who thought she was doing Molly and Luce a favor.

Unfortunately, Molly and Luce hadn't prepared very well for opening a café. Sure, there was plenty of food but there was only Molly working in the kitchen, me as one of the waiters and Isabella at the cash register. Molly had been cooking like crazy all morning with barely a moment to stop. I'd been delivering dishes that were increasingly incorrect, missing elements like no hash brown, or having far too much of one thing and not enough of another, such as an enormous hill of salmon next to a small pile of scrambled egg. We had the idea that every time we'd order a coffee we'd be able to get it from next door, but that wasn't working either because there were too many people going in there, so it was crowded and getting coffees and carrying them through was a dangerous exercise.

Isabella opened the walk-in door and looked in, her face frantic.

"We have to keep going. We are now thirty-five orders behind," she said.

"Okay, we can do this," Molly said.

We rushed back to work and a few minutes later, true to her word, Peta arrived, grabbed an apron and started delivering dishes. It wasn't long however before she realized that the kitchen wasn't doing so well, so she went out there, gave the apron to Molly, and took over cooking duties instead. With Peta cooking and getting the orders right and the three of us delivering food, we soon managed to get things under some semblance of control. The afternoon blurred into platters of food. All I could see was scrambled eggs and sausages, omelets and milkshakes. At one point I splashed coffee down my leg and I don't think I even felt it. I had no time to think, but still somewhere in the back of my mind floating along was a deep and desperate sorrow I had for my cousin. I didn't know exactly what had happened but Will leaving without saying a word couldn't have been good. The fact that Luce refused to speak was even worse.

"You are doing an excellent job girl," I heard a familiar voice say as I put down two plates.

I focused and pulled myself out of the waitressing blur to realize that Henry G and Olivia were sitting at a table.

"Oh, hey, thanks, we try our best," I said.

"This place is kinda nice, like a fifties-style diner, that's the feel," Henry G said, smiling at me. I saw that Olivia was looking at him again with those puppy dog eyes. Was this a date? Why were they out together now?

"I hope you enjoy it. I have to go. Lots of orders," I said. They both said goodbye to me as I rushed off to continue delivering food.

Time blurred on and I didn't see them leave, only realizing they were gone when I was wiping up their table for the next set of customers. I saw a few familiar faces from town, a couple of the shop owners and other people we knew but we didn't have any time to talk, not with all the orders that we had to fill.

Eventually we reached five o'clock and that was when Molly took off her apron and declared they were going be closing. She sent Isabella to the door to turn any more customers away. We finished up making all the orders and then waited for people to finish their meals. We cleaned as the last stragglers ate their food and drank the coffees before departing. The place went from half full to empty in about ten minutes, there being some tipping point as people realized that we were closing up. Molly sent Isabella home and also Julie from next door, before locking both the doors. Molly, Peta and I dragged our exhausted selves through the open archway into *Traveler*. Luce was standing behind the counter, her hair a mess and her face sweaty. At some point there must've an incident with the coffee machine because her face and neck were covered in coffee grinds. She had splattered milk all over her clothing and looked like she had lost a fight with the coffee machine.

We trudged in and the three of us sat down at one of the booths.

"Well there goes day one," Luce murmured.

"You guys made some money but you're going to need some more staff if it keeps up like that," Peta said.

My feet were throbbing, aching like crazy from standing up and rushing around all day and now that I was sitting every muscle in my body was making its protests known. I looked down at myself and realized that I was covered in bits of food as well. At some point I must've been squirted with yellow mustard which had made a streak right down the leg of my black pants. We sat there in silence, all four of us decompressing from the day. Behind Luce the coffee machine muttered to itself in Italian. Who knew what it wanted? Maybe more water or to be cleaned or something else? All four of us were in a stupor quietly staring when there was a bang on the front door of *Traveler* that jolted us awake.

"We're closed," Molly yelled without looking.

"It's me, open up."

All four of us went from half asleep to wide awake. It was Will on the other side of the door. Molly rushed over and unlocked it and Will walked in. He was wearing his landscaping clothes and he looked almost as bad as Luce did. He had dirt under his fingernails, bits of grass all over him and spread up his neck and in his hair, and from the state of his pants it looked he'd fallen in every mud puddle in Harlot Bay. His boots were caked with dirt and his hands had black streaks on them.

Will stopped in the middle of the room and looked at Peta and me sitting in the booth. Molly was frozen by the door watching him.

"Does she know?" Will asked in a low tone.

"She knows," I said. Will looked back at Luce who was standing behind the counter, her face dark with the coffee grinds, biting her lip anxiously.

"I know I went silent last night. I know you think I'm

angry or mad because I went silent and then I left. I don't know why I did that. I think maybe it's something my dad does, so I do it too," Will said.

"It's okay," Luce whispered. Will rushed around the counter and grabbed Luce in a tremendous hug. She started crying and then so was he, tears streaking down his dirty face.

"I'm sorry Luce, I'm sorry I left," he said.

Molly, Peta and I were frozen, stuck in our places. I felt like I was completely still like a statue, only my heart beating wildly.

"There's no space here and that thing's dangerous. Come out here," he said. He led Luce out from behind the counter around to the front of it.

"I've been carrying this for weeks, planning it for even longer and I don't know, maybe this isn't the ideal place to ask, and perhaps we should both have showers and be somewhere nice like a beach or a garden, but I was out working today and mowing lawns and I couldn't stop thinking about you, couldn't stop thinking about *us*, and couldn't stop thinking about our future. I'm covered in grass and dirt because I came straight here as soon as I realized what I wanted. What I wanted to ask you," he said. I heard Molly gasp from behind me. Luce had gone from crying and half smiling to now standing with a shocked look on her face. Her eyes only grew wider as Will knelt down on one knee and reached into the pocket of his coveralls.

"You're kneeling, you're kneeling down," Luce babbled.

"Well, that's what you do when you *ask*," Will said.

"Oh my goddess," I whispered under my breath.

"Shush over there," Will said with a cheeky smile. He took a ring out of his pocket and clasped Luce's hand, one that was covered in coffee grinds from the day's hard labor.

"You're a witch and I love you. Marry me," he said.

It was one of those moments again where all the world seemed to stop and then it jolted forward with tremendous speed. One of those moments where you became aware of gravity, the fact that the planet was spinning and the universe with it, that everything had come perfectly together, falling precisely in order, just for this instant.

"Yes, I'll marry you," Luce said. Will slipped the ring onto her finger and then stood up and kissed her. It was only when they broke apart and he looked towards us that the three of us unfroze, and then the poor boy was nearly crushed to death as we hugged the two of them, squealing and jumping around.

"Oh my goddess, oh my goddess, oh my goddess," Molly said, grinning from ear to ear.

We pulled apart and I found myself covered with not only the food of the day but now coffee grinds from Luce and bits of grass from Will. The moment was intensely happy but as I stood there, seeing Molly hugging Luce again and babbling away, I couldn't help but remember what I'd heard when I'd touched Ollie on the hand yesterday. The sounds of shouting, the sounds of ending. This moment was happy and the future would be too, but I could only hope that what I'd heard was simply a bad moment and that Molly would get to be as happy as Luce was now.

Luce showed me the ring and grinned at me.

"I'm getting married, Harlow. I'm getting married!"

CHAPTER TWELVE

*T*he library was quiet and calming which was exactly what I needed after the past few noisy days. I had about an hour to go before I was finished my late night shift and I would drive around to see Jack. I was exhausted and on a break so I took a sip of water and leaned against the wall, idly flicking through Hans's autobiography. The quiet was sublime and in strict contrast to the many noisy places I'd been recently. Noisy place number one was of course the night Will had proposed to Luce. Eventually we'd all driven back up to the mansion where they told the moms and Aunt Cass their news. This resulted in much squealing and hugging. Will, who was a fairly solid boy from lifting heavy logs and bags of potting mix, was almost crushed to death by three excited witch mothers, and also to my surprise Aunt Cass. She wasn't quite as giddy as the moms, but she did grab Luce in an enormous hug and then Will before kissing him on the cheek and saying "I'm sure you'll scrub up fine for the wedding." It had taken all of a minute flat for the moms to turn to us and ask what *our* marriage plans were?

I owed Molly ten bucks over that one. I'd bet it would be at least five minutes before that particular topic came up. She'd bet one minute.

We'd promptly ignored the moms and taken ourselves back off to our end of the mansion. This was especially also because the protesters were still staying at the Torrent mansion and so all that cheering and squealing had been watched by faces pressed up against windows from above us.

The second noisy place in the list of course, was the theater. Rehearsals had now grown louder, but also tenser. We were now getting down to the sharp and pointy end of it. Previously when someone dropped a line they might laugh and there were plenty of jokes around the rehearsal space. Now everyone was growing more serious. A dropped line was a moment of panic and no one laughed. We were starting to get through entire soliloquies without any problems and you could dimly see that we might actually have a play. But at times it felt as though we were on Truer Island, looking back at the shore and contemplating a long swim.

At rehearsals there was a constant hubbub, people rehearsing and then when dropped lines occurred, people panicking. There were now even more guards looming about the place. It wouldn't be long before we opened and then it would only run for a week before it closed, and everyone was hoping that there would be no more terrible incidents.

The noisy third place would be the *Traveler Cafe*, opened up next to *Traveler*. *Magic Bean* had reopened after beefing up their security which as far as we could tell was small, nondescript security cameras all over the place, and that had taken away some of the business that had flooded Molly and Luce on their very first day of opening. The coffee side of the business was still okay. Luce was working that coffee machine like a mad woman. It was the café side of things that was struggling. It was still Molly, Luce and their three employees, but it simply wasn't enough. I was more than willing to help out but because I was working on the play and then at the library I was exhausted or not available. The same went for Peta. She was still working on the play and promised Molly and Luce that once it was over she would help them out. Although both Molly and Luce were still ecstatically happy, riding that glowing wave of Luce getting engaged, they were returning home completely exhausted and covered in bits of food. They needed to hire more qualified staff and soon, but they were having a little bit of trouble finding anyone who knew how to cook or wait tables properly. There was no shortage of teenagers and unemployed in Harlot Bay but they simply didn't even have the time to train anyone to do the jobs. They needed someone who could land on their feet immediately.

I pulled myself away from the recollection of all the noisy places I was frequenting, took another sip of water and breathed in the delicious silence of the library. It was just me and the papers, and I guess the dust. I turned back to Hans's autobiography and kept idly flicking through it. I honestly don't know why I was bothering to continue reading it. I hadn't finished it by any means, but I thought the chances of finding any clues as to who might have poisoned him were incredibly slim. It turned out I'd been slightly wrong about the autobiography too. At first glance it had been pure ego, stories designed to paint Hans in the most positive light of all. But somehow mixed in there were other tidbits that showed that at one time in his life he'd been a fairly normal and probably, dare say it, good person. I flicked to a page that showed black and white photos from thirty years ago. It was a production of *Much Ado About Nothing* and Hans was the assistant to the director, Viola. This was the show that ended with an explosion and death. Hans and the rest of the cast and crew had taken one serious photo, their faces solemn, and then in the next they'd all pulled ridiculous expressions, sticking out their tongues.

Underneath they listed all of their names but also had made up a variety of fake professions for themselves. Hans was listed as chief snackologist, chips and beer division. Another cast member was listed as a sandwich rustler. The director was junior assistant to the junior herpetologist, and an enormous man with a giant beard was listed as chief lupineologist, which I guess was a joke about the fact that he looked like the Wolf Man. It was hard to see looking at the photo of Hans looking so young and happy that he would turn into the horrible man that I knew, shouting and abusive, short-tempered and cruel.

I checked the time and saw I should be about to get back to work, so I thought I might call Jack but the man obviously knew my break times as well and my phone rang in my hand.

"Hey Jack," I said, waiting for it.

"Harlow Torrent," Jack began, his voice low, his tone serious. "Harlow Torrent, Slip witch will you mar-" He paused for comedic effect and then continued. "Make me the happiest man alive by coming around for a very late dinner?"

"Oh shut up, ha, ha, ha," I said.

Both Ollie and Jack were very well aware of the consequences of Will asking Luce to marry him. It had turned out that the three of them had had *many* conversations privately and knew that as soon as *one* of them took the leap, the thumbscrews would be on for the other two to do the same. So what had these two boys decided to do? Make a hilarious joke about it. Ollie had taken Molly for a walk up into the forest and then had been talking about how much he loved her before suddenly kneeling down. Molly had gasped and then Ollie had merely tied his shoelaces and stood up and said "Shall we continue walking?" Molly had walloped him across the head and then he had laughed like a crazy person.

Jack had done similar things to me, dropping his fork deliberately on the ground and then kneeling down, taking my hand and asking could I help him back up?

Very funny these two boys of ours thought they were.

"So how's the library, how's the quiet?" he asked.

"It's delectable. I think I might get a couple of stacks of paper and just sleep here," I said.

We chatted away for a couple of minutes before Jack's tone really did turn serious this time, and not to make a joke about getting married.

"I have some news on Coldwell and that mall approval that was rushed through. One of the council members rents a home and Coldwell is the landlord. I looked it up and you know what's strange? He's paying far less rent than he normally would for a house like that. It's practically a mansion. The council member and his family only moved in last month. It looks to me that there's some bribery of some kind going on via under market rents but it's going be fairly hard to prove or to get much on it."

"Oh yeah, Coldwell. I'd forgotten about him," I muttered.

"I thought I might secretly pass the information to Carter. I'm going to see if I can gather anything else first. Someone getting a good deal on rent isn't exactly the crazy story of corruption that will bust this thing wide open," Jack said.

We chatted a bit more, talking mostly about Coldwell and Carter, before we finally said goodbye and I returned to the quiet silence of the library.

With everything going on in my life, ranging from the possibility I had a spell cast on me to the fact that we still hadn't caught the magical salamander, my aunt getting married, my cousin getting engaged, and everything that was happening with the play, I honestly didn't care about Sylvester Coldwell or anything that he was doing. Let other people solve how he'd corrupted council members. Maybe when I talked to Jack later, I would suggest he stop chasing it although he probably wouldn't given that although he was no longer a policeman, he still had that instinct to track down bad guys.

I got myself up from the floor, feeling my bones creaking and my muscles aching slightly and returned to my sorting but my mind kept straying. I kept thinking about Coldwell, and then Coldwell's father and his father before him. A while ago we had discovered that Coldwell's great grandfather had bought an orchard after part of it had burned down and then sold it later for a fabulous profit which had helped set the family on their way to fortune and their current real estate dealings. This was a potential crime hidden in the very, very deep past but one that Ollie and I had uncovered through examining property transaction records and newspaper articles.

I guess if we had the time to dig through all these papers we might find other things that could incriminate Sylvester Coldwell himself.

At that thought I remembered the papers that Ollie had been stacking that had been driving him slightly mad. The ones showing a building had been constructed out on Truer Island that apparently didn't exist. The article showing Grandma, Aunt Cass and Hattie all the same age together. In the rush of everything I'd forgotten to take a copy of the article. Even as I realized that, it occurred to me it was very strange that I'd forgotten to take such an obvious thing. I heard that small voice in the back of my mind again.

It's the spell.

I dropped my current task which was sorting school records for two different schools sixty years ago and went to find the piles Ollie had been working on. After a few fruitless minutes of searching I had to conclude that they were no longer there. I quickly rang Ollie.

"Ollie, it's Harlow. Where are all those papers you were working on, the one with that article showing my Grandma, Hattie Stern and Aunt Cass in the ocean swimming? Where is the pile of pay slips for that building out on Truer Island?"

"Oh, they're not there? I didn't move them. Can't you find them?" Ollie said.

The underground room was messy I admit but there was no way Ollie's piles were sitting somewhere that I just happened to glance over and miss.

"Nope, they're not here," I said with a sinking feeling in my stomach.

"I'll have a look tomorrow. They probably were moved, although I don't know who would have done that," Ollie said. I said goodbye and then spent the next ten minutes or so walking around, checking every pile I could find but my first instincts had been right. The papers were gone and I'm sure we wouldn't be seeing them again. I sat back down on the ground and had a drink of water, feeling a sensation that was becoming most unwelcome. It felt like a cold hand on the back of my neck or a fog across my mind. Something was opposing me, something was pushing me and I didn't know *what*.

I checked my watch and saw that somehow I still had half an hour to go, but I made a slightly sneaky executive decision: I was done for the night. I dusted myself off somewhat, locked up the library and then went out to my car, which took a few tries to get started. I was sitting there waiting for it to warm up when I saw a tall lanky familiar figure rushing across the end of the street carrying a large black garbage bag. It was Marcus Fyfe, the music director. He vanished around the corner.

"It's nothing. I mean, yes, he is walking around late at night with a black garbage bag in the middle of town. So that's nothing, right?" I said out loud, hearing how stupid I sounded. I made a split second decision, turned my car off, locked my things inside, and took off running down the street. I skidded around the corner just in time to see Marcus vanish around another corner about three blocks away. There was simply no doubt about it: he was heading in the direction of the theater. I jogged my way down the street, feeling my legs starting to burn and hearing the loud sound of my breath. I think I'd entered that beautiful period for about half an hour where when you exercise you get fitter, but since I'd been forced to cut back training sessions with Kaylee I'd seen my fitness decline to the level of someone who spent all their time lounging on the sofa. By the time I reached the corner I was out of breath. I stopped there and looked around. There were two guards standing out the front of the theater. Since the snake had been released, more guards had been hired and they were on twenty-four-hour watch so no one could go in or out when they weren't meant to. I stood there watching and then noticed a patch of black was moving along. It was Marcus creeping in the shadows, coming up to the abandoned building that adjoined the theater. On both sides of the theater were abandoned buildings, a sad judgment on the economic state of Harlot Bay. I saw Marcus look around and then leap over a small fence, vanishing behind it.

My urge to follow, to chase, was high but I did the sensible thing instead, or at least I tried to. My idiotic phone wasn't cooperating yet again. I couldn't call Jack. I couldn't call Sheriff Hardy. I couldn't call anyone. I banged it in my palm in frustration.

What should I do? I could tell the guards I guess...

I had a few moments of indecision, battling out in my mind between get involved, find out what's going on, and don't be crazy be safe. Eventually I took a deep breath and crossed the road heading in the same direction as Marcus. I crept up to the low fence and then peered over. The building he'd entered had been a haberdasher's at some point in the distant past according to the aged signage above the door. Chances where it had been abandoned for the last twenty years. A window at the front was open.

I climbed over the fence and crept up to the window, listening intently. I could hear footsteps inside, Marcus walking around. Then I did something that I guess was fairly stupid. I took another deep breath and climbed in the window.

I wasn't entirely crazy though; I cast a concealment spell over me. It was heavy and in my tired state took quite a lot of energy but at least Marcus wouldn't be able to spot me even if he looked directly at me.

The inside of the building wasn't completely dark. There were glass skylights in the ceiling still intact, which was incredible for a building of this age. Beams of moonlight came in. Where I'd entered was a small office area, but then the building opened up into a large cavernous factory floor. I crept out of the office area and over near a pillar, hiding in the darkness. It wasn't long before Marcus came walking out of the black no longer carrying the enormous garbage bag.

I pressed myself up against the pillar and watched him go. He was humming to himself as though he was happy about something. It wasn't long before I heard him walk back through the offices and go out the window, closing it behind him. Then I was alone.

I checked my phone again but still no signal. Calling myself a fool about a thousand times I walked further into the building, finding that on the far side there were more offices, a maze of small rooms and corridors much like dressing rooms at the theater. Thinking I was going to come upon a bag of snakes or something like that, I crept around with every muscle tensed. But I didn't find anything. It was too dark to search every room properly, so wherever he put the bag, it was well hidden.

My internal timer of *well, that's enough crazy Harlow* hit its limit and so I decided to get out of there. I went back the way I came, across the large empty floor as quietly as I could, opened the window and climbed back out before closing it behind me. I took a quick look over the fence before jumping it and rushing back the way I came to my car. It was only once I got back there that my phone decided to start working again. I decided after doing something so ridiculously foolish that I would do something sensible and called Sheriff Hardy on his private number.

"Harlow, what is it?" Sheriff Hardy said, sleep blurring his voice.

I checked the time, it was only just nine o'clock. Was he in bed already?

"Oh, sorry to wake you."

"I've been working too many hours so I had to go to bed early. What can I help you with?" I heard a voice in the background say something to him. It was Aunt Ro. I guess they were both staying at his house. And in that moment, as absurd as it might sound, I realized that after they'd marry she'd probably be moving out to live with him. Hot on the heels of that realization was another: Luce would be moving out too. It was like a timer had begun between a ring and then a wedding and then eventually I would no longer be living with my cousins. Would we all scatter to the four winds, leaving Torrent mansion empty?

"Harlow, what was it? I need to sleep," Sheriff Hardy said.

"Oh, sorry, um, I just saw Marcus Fyfe, the music director, break into an empty building that was next to the theater. I don't know why," I told Sheriff Hardy.

That certainly got his attention. He asked me to repeat my story and although I wanted to hide parts of it and just say that I'd stayed across the street, I told the Sheriff that I'd followed him inside and crept around, but I hadn't seen where he'd placed the bag. At this Sheriff Hardy made a few judgmental noises but didn't say anything else. In the end he thanked me and told me he would send some of his men over before wishing me a good night.

As I drove over to Jack's I certainly hoped that it was a good night although there was sadness as well. Was Marcus possibly the culprit? He seemed so happy and carefree. He was always making jokes with the teenagers and he could play any song apparently ever written. He would keep them entertained by playing their favorite TV theme songs, and I think he practically had a theme for every single one of them if he saw them walking by. He was one of those people that in the midst of panic would be able to calm everyone down just by playing something on his piano, charming teenagers the way he might charm a wild animal. So over to Jack I drove with a mixture of sadness and partially relief. Hopefully the police would find something and then they would question Marcus and I guess it might all be over. Then all I had to contend with was helping Aunt Cass find the salamander, Aunt Ro getting married, and everything else that was going on in my life.

I arrived at Jack's and saw the warm glow of the light in the front window. Feeling my spirits lift with every step towards his front door, I soon forgot about Marcus and went inside to see my lovely boyfriend and spend some time with a delicious hot cup of cocoa.

CHAPTER THIRTEEN

I was almost late to rehearsal the next day after having a difficult time dragging myself out of Jack's incredibly warm bed.

I was surprised to find Marcus sitting behind the piano playing one of the opening songs as a warm up.

Why was he here? Surely Sheriff Hardy hadn't had his men investigate the building next door and clear him already? I immediately rang Sheriff Hardy, but he didn't answer. Before I could worry about exactly what was going on, I was called into the rehearsal by the director.

"Let's go, let's go, let's go, everyone," Emilion yelled out.

Aunt Cass was there, although not in her complete makeup. Like some others, she'd only show up for the first rehearsal, perform her lines and then leave to go to work.

I was immediately pressed into service helping out with costumes. I whispered a quick hello to Peta and Henry G and we got started. I didn't have time to worry about what exactly was going on with Marcus and the police once the rehearsals began. My job was essentially a roving dogsbody to help out wherever help was needed. At the beginning that was the costumes as there were some quick changes. Later on it quieted down and I even had some free time backstage which you'd think is a relief but was quite anxiety inducing. I often felt that I was standing around, useless, not helping at all, and so most of the time I would head out to the dressing rooms to bust any teenagers up to anything and make sure they were all aware of their times and when they were to go back on stage. There had been more than once that an entrance had been missed because the teenager in question was making out in a dressing room.

We hit that ten minutes and so I walked down to the dressing rooms, opening doors as I went and rushing teenagers out wherever I saw them. I came to Emilion's dressing room (he was using the room Hans was poisoned in) and on impulse opened the door. Normally no one was stupid enough to hide out in here when Hans was the director, but Emilion was much more cheerful, so maybe some teenagers thought he was much more lenient.

I stepped inside the dressing room and closed the door behind me, looking around. Emilion hadn't done much to change the dressing room in his time here. It still looked pretty much the way Hans had left it. The only real difference was there was an enormous vase of flowers sitting on the main desk. I walked over to the desk vaguely aware that I was no longer searching for teenagers, but perhaps snooping? I saw on the desk there was a copy of Hans's autobiography. It was open to the middle, an egotistical story of how Hans single-handedly saved some production of *Macbeth* ten years ago. The way it was told you would think that he was the director, the cast, the lighting assistants, the musicians, and everyone all in one.

I looked across the desk and saw an envelope that was torn open addressed to Emilion. I picked it up and saw the return address on the back was the Harlot Bay Hospital.

Without really thinking about it I opened the envelope and took out the note inside:

Don't get too comfortable. I'll be back soon – Hans.

That was all it said. I slipped the note back into the envelope and put it on the desk.

Was Hans coming back? Oh goddess, please, *no.*

I realized that I was standing in quite a bad position if someone were to open the dressing room door. This was no longer merely looking for teenagers, but actively snooping through the director's things. I turned about-face and went outside, closing the door behind me. I then rushed back to the stage to continue helping out. I had rehearsed so many of these costume changes that felt like I was working on automatic, which gave my mind time to free roam. The information that Hans would be returning was certainly unwelcome. But was he really? I'd heard he had woken up and that he knew he'd been poisoned, but perhaps it was just the type of egotistical note that Hans would send someone to keep them on edge, to make them know that they weren't really in charge, that *he* was.

We finished the rehearsal almost on time. We were still running a little long, the teenagers not quite up to speed with their lines, the costume changes not going smoothly, but you could feel we were getting closer. Esmeralda called for a ten-minute break before we'd go again. I took myself to the kitchen to get a glass of water and realized I had completely forgotten about last night until Marcus appeared with a cup of coffee in his hand.

"How goes it, Harlow? Still reading that autobiography?" he asked.

"I gave up. It's mostly egotistical stuff," I said. I took a hasty sip of my water and looked around, glad that there were other people in the kitchen so that I wasn't alone. Even as I thought *that* I felt guilty. There was just no way that

Marcus could have been the one to release a snake or poison Hans. He was too kind!

"Hey did I see your car last night outside the library?" Marcus asked.

"I have a part-time job working there. I'm sorting papers that are getting digitized," I said. I didn't want to be in this conversation. I half expected him to say *oh, so was that what you were meant to be doing when you were following me instead?*

"I think about getting a stable job sometimes. It would be a lot better than working for Hans," Marcus said. He finished his coffee, rinsed his cup and walked back to his piano after giving me a smile.

I was still watching him go when Kira appeared next to me.

"I know he's tall and lanky, but you do have Jack you know," she said punching me in the arm.

I punched her in the arm in return.

"It may surprise you but adults can talk to other adults without getting a crush on them, unlike certain teenagers."

"Ouch hit me right where it hurts," Kira said miming a pain over her heart.

"I'll tell you about it later," I said to her in an undertone.

"Oooh more mysterious shenanigans, I guess," Kira said and winked back at me. Then her demeanor changed. She went from the Kira I knew, a witty and sometimes sarcastic teenager, to blushing pink and fumbling with the glass in her hand. I looked up and saw that Fox, the teenager who I'd caught crying in the dressing room a few days ago, had come into the kitchen. I could feel Kira's whole body tense up as he came over near the sink and filled up a glass of water. Fox glanced at me and pointedly did not glance at Kira, seeming too embarrassed to look at her.

"Hi Harlow," he mumbled. Then, in a quieter voice, he said "Hi Kira."

Kira's face turned bright pink again and she mumbled something back that probably was a greeting. I don't know, I think I was losing my ability to speak teenager. Fox gulped down his glass of water in record time and then bolted out of there. It was only once he was gone that Kira let out a breath that she seemed to be holding.

Despite everything that was going on I was not one to let such an opportunity pass.

"Kira's got a boyfriend," I teased.

"Shut up, I do not," Kira said and punched me in the arm again.

"You want to marry him. You want to have his little Fox babies," I said.

"I do not. I just want to, I don't know, talk to him or something," Kira said. She bit her lip when she said "something" and I understood, of course, that the *something* that she wanted to be doing with him did not involve talking.

"I saw you at a party, Kira Stern, yelling out to some guy and talking to him. Why can't you just talk to Fox?"

"I don't know, it's just he's so cute and my whole body freezes and I don't know what's going on," Kira said. We didn't get to talk anymore because Esmeralda called that the ten-minute break was over and we were to get back to rehearsals. We went again, another full rehearsal rushing through, although this time there was a stand-in for Aunt Cass, who had gone off to work. We reached the end of that one and there was a groan from the cast as Esmeralda called out we'd be taking a short break before going once more. In the break I checked my phone and saw that Sheriff Hardy had rung me back. I called him and surprisingly he picked up on the first ring.

"Hey, Harlow, I thought I'd call you to tell you some information we've uncovered," he began.

"Did you talk to Marcus?" I whispered into the phone, unable to stop myself.

"We're looking into it. I can't tell you any more. Okay?"

"Okay, fine," I said.

"They're looking into the poison that Hans was poisoned with. It's not any of the standard ones. It's something exotic so sent it off to a toxicologist in the city. My bet is given that we found a venomous snake it was probably going to be something like that," he said.

"Right, so do we need to look for someone who owns snakes?" I asked.

"Yes, we're going to be investigating that. I thought I'd let you know in case that was useful information for you," Sheriff Hardy said.

He obviously couldn't say more. I guessed he was still at work and had to be talking in code. What he'd really been saying was venomous snakes are involved and I know you're investigating so be careful. I had to end the call because soon we were back into rehearsals again.

We were halfway through rehearsal in a complicated costume change, me and Henry G and Peta pulling costumes off teenagers and grabbing other ones when there was an enormous splat right next to us, and I was splashed with water.

The three of us had the barest moment of realization before water bombs cascaded down on us from the rafters above, exploding on the stage and drenching all three of us. From high above came the laughter of teenagers thinking their prank was the funniest thing in the history of time. I didn't laugh and neither did Peta, but I think that was maybe just shock. There had been quite a few pranks in the early days of rehearsals, but they had faded away as well as we'd all become more serious. Henry G *definitely* didn't laugh. He shrieked out loud, which became a yell, and then he cursed and ran off stage swearing, holding his face as though he'd been doused with acid rather than water. Everyone in the theater had laughed initially at us getting drenched, but seeing Henry G, who was normally witty and laughing swear out loud and run off had caused a pall of silence to fall across the theater.

"Okay everyone, let's clean up the water and no more pranks, not at least until we're finished," Emilion said. The three teenagers involved with it came down from the gantry and I gave a double blink at what they were carrying: it was an empty black garbage bag. It appeared the same as the one Marcus had been carrying yesterday. Was this what he'd been doing? Somehow sneaking in a bag full of water balloons, maybe from next door? As with a lot of the old buildings in Harlot Bay there were plenty of secret tunnels and secret doors. Maybe Marcus had found a way into the theater to bypass the guards. But why would he bother, just for a practical joke like this?

The rehearsal paused while they dried up the stage and took the costumes off that would need to be dried as well. The teenagers got a bit of a dressing down from the director, although it wasn't that bad, certainly not as bad as what Hans would've done. It was mainly around the fact that the costumes were now wet and as they were unique items created specifically for the play, we didn't have backups if they became damaged.

I went down to the dressing room to find a towel, Peta following close behind me, water dripping off her clothing. I dried myself and then went and knocked on Henry G's door. When there was no answer I opened it, only to find his dressing room was empty. There was a wet patch on the floor on the carpet where he'd obviously come in but Henry G was nowhere to be found. I closed his dressing room door and went back out to the rehearsal space, looking around to see if I could find him but he simply wasn't there. Eventually we continued rehearsals, absent Henry G, who only returned an hour and a half later in a set of new clothes, smiling at everyone, and waggling his fingers at the teenagers who had doused us.

"Oh, you got me, you naughty little urchins," he said to them. I couldn't help but feel it was a pretense. The look on his face when he'd been doused with the water balloons was one of pure rage, of anger, and perhaps fear as well.

I didn't have time to think about these things, of course. Our third rehearsal soon flowed into the fourth and it was just a blur of Shakespeare and the *Taming of the Shrew* over and over again.

CHAPTER FOURTEEN

*T*here was a layer of dust at least an inch thick over my poor neglected office. The early morning rays of the sun were shining in the window showing me just exactly how poor and neglected my office was. I put down my laptop, raising a cloud of dust which I waved away with my hand. I had a rare morning off. A large part of the set was being built today so rehearsals were only starting after lunch. I decided on a whim and also after waking up ridiculously early for no good reason at all to come into my office in the hope that I would see John Smith and possibly to do some research. I'd lingered outside on the sidewalk looking around hoping I would see John. When I hadn't, I'd unlocked the office and come upstairs. Usually when I was in my office, he would turn up, I think sometimes being drawn here, because he definitely had no memory for when appointments were meant to take place.

It had been odd walking up the stairs. They creaked in that familiar way but it felt like returning to your high school a year after you've graduated. Everything looks smaller, both familiar yet strange at the same time.

I opened the small fridge, held my nose, and threw out the milk that was on the verge of becoming sentient and starting a small chain of restaurants. I washed out my dusty mug and settled for a black coffee as I sat down at my old desk and turned my laptop on. As I waited I had a look through the papers that Ollie had given me. It was all the research he'd done on acapella groups. If John appeared I was going to go through them with him in the hope that something would trigger a memory and perhaps I could find out who he was. Given how I'd failed to discover anything about John so consistently over the years I didn't have high hopes for this venture but I had to try.

Yes okay, *some* of it was guilt. When I'd taken the job with the theater, it's not like I'd exactly had a going away party where I'd told John I was leaving. I was committed to helping him. I found it sad that he was dead and couldn't move on, couldn't accept that he was gone. But that's the thing with ghosts. They're not *alive*. They're not *here*. Their problems are all over. Compared to snakes being let loose in a theater, directors been poisoned, and magical salamanders roaming the town causing love and hatred everywhere they went, it was easy to put the problems of a ghost aside.

My laptop started up and I headed out to the internet. I shuffled aside all the papers and found the program for the *Taming of the Shrew*. They'd recently been printed and I'd snagged myself a copy because it listed every cast member and person who was working on the production, both first and last names. I was going to look through every one to see if there was any possible distant connection or clue I could find.

I had to admit that I was doing this also because I was a touch embarrassed about what had occurred with Marcus. I'd spoken with Sheriff Hardy who had told me they'd questioned Marcus who had readily confessed that he'd smuggled in a black bag full of water balloons through a secret passage he had discovered. It had all been for a prank, a joke on Henry G. Marcus hadn't been doing anything suspicious at all. After discovering that it had all been for a prank I'd felt incredibly guilty that I had doubted him in the first place. My instincts had told me that he couldn't have been doing anything, but I'd ignored them and although I hadn't done much except for tell Sheriff Hardy, who had then done the right thing to interview him to discover the truth, I still felt like I'd accused him directly.

I opened up the program and started looking down the list of names. I was going to check everyone who worked with Hans first and then move on to locals, given that I was fairly certain that although a local might hate Hans, they wouldn't have the kind of hatred that would lead them to poison him and then releasing a snake in the theater as well as cutting sandbags.

Being that I had recently accused Marcus, he was on my mind so I decided to look him up first. The internet quickly returned parts of his history. I found a record of him being a jazz pianist in New York, working in different bars. He'd been a musical director for a small children's play and then started appearing firstly as a piano player for Hans and then moving up to music director. I also found a grinning photo of him, his arm wrapped around some beautiful blonde girl who was wearing a bikini. They were on a beach somewhere. Although he was grinning in the picture, I felt like he was staring at me and saying "Me? Really? You thought it was *me* who would do those things?" I quickly closed it and moved on to the next name.

I settled on Olivia, the woman who we were fairly sure was in love with Henry G. Her full name was Olivia Knapp, born and raised in Fort Lauderdale in Florida. I found an old graduation photo, some social media accounts, and then the next trace of her is when she started working for Hans years ago, simply listed as an assistant. There was nothing there to find. I continued going through the list but it was becoming increasingly clear that this was a futile task. Some people simply didn't have anything on the Internet. It was as though they just appeared out of nowhere, or they had names that were so common that there were thousands of them.

Henry G was listed only as Henry G on the program so I couldn't get his last name. Under Henry G, he first appeared working a year ago as a costume designer for Hans and then in his subsequent productions.

I was about to give up my searching when I felt a furry shape brush past my legs and Adams emerged from under the desk carrying a thick rolled up catalog in his mouth. He jumped up on the desk and dropped it with a thud.

"Page forty-one. I want you to buy it for me," he said and then proceeded to have a bath, as though all he had to do was give me the instruction.

"Good morning Adams. How are you today?" I said sarcastically.

"I'm okay, I want you to buy me the collar on page forty-one though," he said, the sarcasm whooshing right over his head.

I opened to the page to find a diamond-studded collar priced at eight thousand dollars.

"Whoa buddy, I can't afford eight thousand dollars! Besides, you don't wear collars anyway. What do you want it for?" I said.

"Page one-two-eight then," Adams said through a mouthful of fur.

I turned to find a much cheaper collar. This one was $29.99 plus shipping and instead of diamonds was diamantes.

"Can I have that one? I feel like you owe me for that time

I saved everyone's lives," Adams said with a crafty look on his face.

"It is true that we owe you but we've paid off that debt with a lot of tuna and a lot of milk and the fact that you get to sleep in our house where it's warm. Again, why do you want a collar? You don't wear them," I asked.

I scratched him under the neck. He held still for a moment before nipping me on the hand and jumping off onto the floor, raising a small cloud of dust as he landed. He began walking around, examining the room as though he'd never seen it before.

"If you just gave me pocket money then I wouldn't have to explain myself," he said, quite sulkily.

I looked back at the page. The collar he was requesting was quite feminine, not something a male black cat would probably wear. A few other memories jolted together. Adams taking food and very carefully carrying it in his mouth rather than hogging it down like he normally did. Oh no, did my cat have a girlfriend? Oh no, was I going to have to have a conversation about *dating* with my cat? "

"So can I have it?" Adams demanded.

"Um, yeah sure I'll order it for you," I said, still working through my thoughts on what exactly I would say to Adams about the responsibilities of having a girlfriend and how that might work.

"That's a nice collar," John Smith said from beside me, appearing.

"Arrrh!" I yelped. Adams took this opportunity to vanish. By the time I calmed down John had sat on the sofa and was smiling at me.

"How are you today, Harlow?" he asked.

"I'm... well, I think I'm good. I think my cat has a girl-friend and there's a lot of other stuff going on right now, but yeah, I think I'll be okay," I blabbered. My sudden suspicion that Adams might have a girlfriend had made the world twist. It was like finding out he was a secret racecar driver or something. It changed my whole conception of how the world *was*. I sipped the last remnants of my now cold black coffee and gathered my thoughts. At least on the good side of the morning John Smith remembered who I was. He'd just deposited a fresh twenty dollar note on the desk, I guess when he'd arrived, so I suppose he assumed that we were going to be having a therapy session now. Before I could launch into going through the list John spoke first.

"I'm looking forward to seeing the *Taming of the Shrew*. They're building the set now. It looks amazing," John said, quite enthusiastic.

"You've been down at the theater?" I asked.

"Oh yes, I've roamed around there many times, through all the dressing rooms, backstage, underneath, it's a wonderful place full of history," John said.

"Underneath? Do you mean immediately underneath the stage where they store props and things?" I asked.

"Props for what?" John Smith said.

I sighed. He was already forgetting. But I continued anyway.

"You said you'd been underneath the theater. Into the floors underneath?" I asked.

"Which theater?" John asked confused.

I made myself another coffee and let go of that line of questioning.

"I want to go through this list of names and articles. Can you see if you recognize anything?" I told John.

I laid out the papers on my very dusty desk, putting my laptop to the side. Although John had at times some very limited interaction with the world, usually just enough to change the channel on the television that he would some-times watch, today it seemed he had almost no influence at all. I had to turn the pages for him as he slowly read through names and the articles. It didn't take long at all and, sadly, as I expected, yielded zero information.

"Are we going to see a singing group?" John said, reading the last article that was about a singing competition which had taken place in 1954.

"No, not right now," I said.

"Well we can't go right now, I mean that's not until next year," John said, touching the article with a ghostly finger.

I felt a small spark of hope. So did that mean that John thought it was currently 1953? Before I could ask him another question though he simply vanished. There was no pop, no rush of cold air, nothing. He didn't say anything. He was just gone, leaving me alone with the papers.

I opened my laptop and the file I'd been keeping on John Smith and quickly wrote down what he'd said about the competition being next year and that perhaps he thought he was in 1953. Again it was the longest of long shots but it was one of the first times I'd managed to tie him to any year at all. I gathered up all the papers and stuffed them in my bag and then took a quick look at the time. It was only just past nine in the morning, although it felt like I'd been at the office for hours. I quickly ordered the collar online for Adams, to get that job out of the way.

I looked at my dust covered office and realized there was another place that I'd abandoned and hadn't been back to in quite a while: my so-called lair up behind the mansion. It was still a few hours until I had to go into rehearsals so I packed my stuff, locked the office, and drove home. The mansion was empty when I got there. Aunt Cass was probably at the *Chili Challenge*, the moms were at the bakery, and even the protesters had departed in their orange bus, probably parking it outside the theater. Molly and Luce weren't home either, having left for work. The day was warming up nicely and there were a few butterflies fluttering madly about the place as I walked up around behind the mansion and into the forest. I soon came to the cottage that I was using, unlocked it and went inside to find it much like my office. There was a layer of dust over everything. It wasn't quite an inch thick but it was there nonetheless. I put my things down and then stood back to have a look at the wall of crazy. Yep, it was still crazy.

I sat down at the small desk, pulled out my laptop and various bits of paper, but then ended up sitting there, blankly staring at the wall. It wasn't for long though because I quickly realized I was staring, and honestly, if I were going to do that, I'd simply go back to the mansion and watch television. I decided I would pin the play program on another wall, and perhaps start writing down some ideas about what exactly was going on with the snake being released and the sandbags and the poison. I opened the drawer of the desk and rummaged around to see if I could find some pins. I found Juliet Stern's journal instead.

I pulled it out and sat back in my chair and started idly flicking through it again. It was a curious thing. I had read every page, or so I'd thought, and most of the time they were mundane - lists of eggs and flour and ingredients for brewing beer. It was essentially the journal of The Merchant Arms, the establishment that Juliet was running. But occasionally I would turn a page and there would be an entry that I'd never seen before. This is what had happened months ago when not only had I been reading an entry about Juliet and some unnamed ancestor of mine hunting the Shadow Witch, but I'd been pulled into a memory, riding along with it, seeing in the memory my daughter Rosetta almost die, and Juliet's daughter actually die at the hands of the Shadow Witch who pushed her spirit out of her body and stole it for herself.

I flicked through the pages, seeing only lists of eggs and hops and other ingredients, a shipment of barrels that had arrived, notes about some of them being sent off to the caves for fermentation before I turned a page and felt a tingle of magic in my fingertips. It was another magical entry, the only one on the entire page.

Torrent continues the hunt without me. Baby will arrive soon. Benjamin is collecting water snails for the pain.

That was all it said and I stared at it, burning the message into my mind. Torrent was obviously my ancestor out on the hunt alone, but the baby arriving soon? Was this an early entry from years past with Juliet talking about her daughter who I'd witnessed being killed by the Shadow Witch? Or was it later on? Had Juliet had another child?

And who was Benjamin? A husband, a relative?

I grabbed a piece of paper and wrote down the entry on it so I wouldn't forget and then pinned it up on the wall.

At least now that I had the name Benjamin I could give that to Ollie and see if he could dig up anything. I flicked back through the journal again hoping another page would open up but none did, and not only that, the entry I had just read vanished, the pages seemingly disappearing from the journal.

I looked up at the wall. There amongst the tangle of strings and newspaper clippings and other things I'd pinned up was a small card that I'd nearly overlapped. I could only see the last few letters of the word Stern, but I knew what the card said. It told me to *visit Hattie Stern*, something I'd promised to do but then had avoided.

I sat there looking at the journal, willing myself to get up, to take it back to my car, to drive out to Hattie's, to tell her that it wasn't just a journal of eggs and bread, but one detailing that her ancestor Juliet had at least at one stage been hunting witches and perhaps other supernatural things.

That she'd had another baby possibly. Maybe Hattie knew who Benjamin was or could shed some light on the subject.

But on the other hand, perhaps the entries were only intended for *me*. Perhaps the journal would only show it to someone it trusted and if I went to see Hattie I would learn nothing more about the past. It would remain opaque to me. I should continue to dig on my own, to visit my lair and look for holes.

Should I trust Hattie? How was I to know the journal entries were truthful? I knew that she was an enormously powerful witch and yes, although the journal had proved useful that could be a trick for something far worse to come.

I put the journal down, my mind swirling with confusion and conflicting desires, and made an abrupt decision to go outside to get away from the wall of crazy and the journal. I walked away from the cottage until I found a grassy area with warm sun beaming. Nearby were the remnants of another old cottage that seriously looked like it had been exploded in the past. There were large bricks and cobblestones scattered all over the place, some of them buried in the earth, grass growing over them. I sat there in the sun with my eyes closed, feeling the warmth of it beating down on me, and took long slow breaths. For some reason the salamander came to mind. Jack and I had been out again collecting water samples for Aunt Cass, and I'd been out with Molly and Luce on another night, definitely burning the candle at both ends. After we broke into the *Magic Bean* and setting off the alarm and then being subsequently warned by Sheriff Hardy, my cousins hadn't mentioned the *Magic Bean* and their so-called magic sandwiches again. With them opening up the *Traveler Cafe* they were both too exhausted to talk when they came home, although I was sure that they were still planning to do something about discovering magic in the mayonnaise. I can tell you this: going down into stormwater drains to collect water samples late at night certainly wasn't the kind of magical glamorous thing you might think a witch would be doing. It was dirty and, frankly, boring. Aunt Cass was adding the strips to her water map but every time we asked if we'd had enough to find where the salamander had made its nest, she told us just to keep collecting samples and she'd let us know.

It wasn't exciting at all and it seemed to me the end of that particular adventure would simply be Aunt Cass going down to the drains and then emerging with some little lizard creature stuffed in a cage or something like that. It would be good to take it away from Harlot Bay, given it was possibly causing love everywhere.

I opened my eyes and looked up to the beautiful blue sky above me. It wouldn't be long before I'd have to get going to go back to rehearsal. The morning had raised more questions than it had answered and I felt adrift, floating along with no particular direction. Once again, I realized that much like working as a police officer, there was only so far an investigation could take you and then the rest of the time was often just waiting for something to happen, hoping you would catch someone in the act, that there would be a witness, that there would be some new development.

I looked back at the wrecked cottage and the scattered stones, following the trail of them to one that was sitting near my feet. There was moss growing on it and at some point in the past, someone had carved the word 'LOST' into the stone. It was the perfect description of how I felt right now. I leaned forward and patted the stone, feeling it was slightly warm from the sun.

"You and me both, buddy," I told the stone.

CHAPTER FIFTEEN

"*I* kind of wish they hadn't changed the name. In my memory it's Cool Blades and it's going to stay Cool Blades forever. The place you take boys and then you kiss them," Peta said, putting her hands on hips and sighing, looking up at the giant glowing sign that now read *Harlot Bay Ice-Skating Rink and Entertainment Center.*

"Oh, really? The place to take boys and kiss them? How many boys have you kissed here?" Jonas asked, poking Peta in the ribs.

"Ah memories," Peta said, laughing.

Jack got out of the car and we all walked up to the doors of the newly rebuilt ice-skating rink. It had been under reconstruction for quite some time, but it finally reopened just a few days ago. Between the theater and Jack working doing carpentry, the protesters at the mansion, and everything else that was going on, it seemed like the last couple of days had gone by in a blur.

I had completely forgotten that we had planned to come ice-skating until Jack had reminded me.

Standing in front of the newly refurbished ice-skating

rink I felt a familiar relaxation come over me. Yes, the outside did look different, the old buzzing sign proclaiming Cool Blades that only worked about fifty percent of the time was gone and I'm sure the inside was different too, but there was a familiarity to it. During summers we'd practically lived at the ice-skating rink, being one of the coolest places literally and figuratively to hang out.

"So is that your plan too? Take me here, kiss me, add me to your list of conquests at the ice-skating rink?" Jack asked, poking me in the ribs too. "How many boys have you added to your list here?"

I grabbed him by the hand and pulled him inside the doors, Jonas and Peta following, and then turned around and planted a kiss on his lips.

"Just one. There we go, you're the only boy I've kissed here," I said.

"What are you talking about, Torrent? There was Ben, there was Ryan, what was that guy with the red hair called?" Peta said.

I gave her poke in the stomach.

"Lists of names are not helpful here because I also have a list of names myself that I could start reading out couldn't I? Like Stephen or Anthony or that guy who had a mustache, even though he was fourteen," I said.

We went into the ice-skating rink and paid at the new and improved counter, which was shiny and beautiful, as opposed to the way it had been in the past, which was old and rundown with various unidentified stains on it. The chill of the room was quite relaxing.

We paid for our skates and then sat down on the staggered benches, lacing them up.

"So you two think you can out-skate us?" I asked Jack and Jonas.

"Definitely," Jonas said.

"Absolutely no doubt about it. After all, we grew up in Canada and up there it's the law. You have to skate or you get a very polite telling off," Jack said.

"When we get out there, let's have a race," Peta said. "Loser buys the snacks."

"I hope you brought some money coz I'm in the mood for about ten hotdogs," Jack said.

I stepped onto the ice and gave a few tentative pushes. It had been awhile, but the muscle memory was still there, and I soon found my groove, gracefully sliding across the ice. When they'd renovated Cool Blades, they'd gone top to bottom. The ice-skating rink was much larger, the seating was better, and off to the side were large double doors the led out to a multi-room entertainment area. There were three birthday parties taking place out there already.

Jack skated up beside me and took my hand. We did a couple of laps, dodging around slower people, not talking and just enjoying the old music that was playing and the atmosphere.

Just last night as Jack and I had laid in bed, both of us fairly exhausted, he suggested in a quiet voice that perhaps nothing else was going to happen to the production, that whoever it was had been scared off by the guards and maybe now it was just time to focus on how both of us wanted to live. It was a sort of odd conversation. I was too sleepy to get much into it, but I realized Jack wasn't merely talking about what we should do in the next few days but was starting a longer conversation that was really about what we were to do together *over the rest of our life*.

It's the funny thing about engagements and relationships - although there were times when an engagement came as a surprise, the fact was that most of the time there had been a lot of conversation leading up to it. Even Luce had admitted that she and Will had talked around topics such as *what kind of house do you think you'd want to live in* without actually saying what kind of house do you want to live in *with me?* Molly and Ollie had done the same. It was that slow movement as two lives came close together and began integrating. First, you start leaving clothes at their house and then you had a cup and a toothbrush, and soon you knew where their towels lived and you were washing the dishes. As I skated with Jack around the rink, honestly it sounded quite delightful.

"Okay, are you suckers ready to lose?" Peta asked, skating up behind us.

"Three laps from the red pole, loser buys the food," I said.

I let go of Jack's hand and took my place next to Peta. We zoomed around another lap until we passed the red pole that was on the side of the rink, and then we took off. There were a few people on the rink, but it was mostly clear, the party-goers still out eating cake.

"Ha, ha, we're gonna win!" I called out as Peta and I took off, opening up a lead. Our glee only lasted about half a lap before Jack and Jonas blurred past us like they'd been shot out of a canon. They sprinted, zipping down the straight and around the bend and coming up around again. Both of us went as fast as we could and I admit we put on a pretty good show to try to keep up, but by the time Jack and Jonas passed the finish line we were almost three-quarters of a lap behind. Peta and I slid past the red pole in disbelief. When we'd been teenagers we'd pulled this game plenty of times on teenage boys, racing them and the loser had to buy the food. We were so good that I don't think either of us ever had to pay for a hot dog or a plate of nachos at Cool Blades.

We slid to a stop by the boys. Jack and Jonas were leaning up against the wall, chatting to each other as though no big deal, we weren't just racing at high speed.

"I want to see those ice skates, see if they're regulation," Peta said, pointing a finger at Jonas.

"I think the two of you are on performance enhancing drugs. You were raised in Canada weren't you? You're on performance enhancing Maple syrup or something," I said.

We gave our respective boyfriends kisses and mucked around before heading out for more skating. Eventually the rink grew more crowded as some of the parties finished up cutting cake and teenagers and children streamed out onto the ice. We eventually slid off, took off our skates, and headed over to the snack bar where we ordered nachos drenched in cheese served with guacamole and jalapeno, and also a round of sodas.

Soon we were sitting at one of the booths eating the food and reminiscing about what Cool Blades had been like when we were teenagers. Jack and Jonas told us they'd had a similar place that they had gone to throughout their childhood and teenage years although they declined to elaborate exactly how many girls *they* had kissed there.

We ate and talked, the topics gradually straying onto work and other adult things. Although it felt we were somewhat reliving our teenage past, the teenage topics of who was kissing whom or what was going on at school weren't of interest to us. Peta and I talked a bit about the play but then we started talking to Jonas about his real estate development business.

"I get the feeling that someone is actively trying to stop me developing the Governor's mansion and I'll give you two guesses who I think it is," Jonas said.

"Does his name rhyme with Moldwell?" I said and then Peta and I snickered.

"Got it in one. I swear that guy must have the dirt on everyone in a position of power in this town," Jonas said.

Jonas had been working for months to develop the

Governor's mansion that was out on Truer Island. The building was in that weird limbo where it was slowly aging and breaking down and it was important historically and should be saved, but at the same time people feared development because it might ruin something... that time was slowly ruining anyway. Jonas had put in plans to restore the mansion and to open it as a museum with a small attached gift shop, and possibly even rent out some of the rooms as a bed-and-breakfast. It was a fairly uncontroversial plan and one that would certainly save the mansion from ruin, but it seems he had been stymied along the way by councilors bringing up odd objections like *what would he do to stop guests breaking windows?*

We continued talking about his business and Coldwell and eventually got to the mall which had been rushed through. Jack had told Jonas that he discovered one of the councilors had moved into a quite nice house at quite a low rent that was owned by Coldwell so Jonas knew there was possibly some bribery taking place. As we started talking about the mall though, Jonas went from fairly cheerful to spiking angry.

"The guy's gonna ruin Harlot Bay. There's no way a mall is going to be good for any business whatsoever. There's just not the population. It's going to be a disaster," he said, dipping his nacho chip so fast into the cheese it snapped off.

"If it's approved does that mean it's just going to go ahead or is there something you can do about it?" I asked.

"Sure, there are a lot of things we can do about it, but honestly, Coldwell needs to be beaten with an iron bar and forced to stop," Jonas said.

Peta and I shared a glance. Jonas didn't sound like he was joking. There was the slightest moment of awkward pause.

"Or we could not threaten to kill the rival real estate developer," Jack said, trying to make a joke.

Jonas sighed and then took a sip of his soda. "It's a joke... the guy just makes me angry. I've dealt with people like him so many times, slippery and slimy, and they always work outside the law. It makes it hard to be a legitimate developer because no one trusts you. If Coldwell was developing the Governor's mansion, you can guarantee he would tell them he would keep it the way it was and then he would ruin it, and then afterward say whoops, sorry, and not care one bit. I mean, I presented a plan where we'd be using locally recovered hardwood from buildings of the same age that had been knocked down so that we could keep it precisely the way it was. Anyway, let's stop talking about that guy and get back out on the ice," Jonas said.

We all agreed with that, finished up our meal, and headed back out onto the ice for more skating. I quickly forgot about Coldwell, the rhythmic motion of pushing myself across the ice soothing me. Despite the music and the chattering teenagers around me, it felt quiet and cool, like sitting in the library amongst the papers. It seemed the last weeks had been a rush of increasing madness and with Aunt Ro and Sheriff Hardy's wedding quickly approaching, the protesters staying at the Torrent mansion and everything else, I knew as soon as I left I would return to that madness. But for the meantime I was content to skate and not think about it.

Jack came up beside me and took my hand.

"You know, he's not serious about that. He wouldn't hurt a fly," Jack said.

"I know. Besides, I don't entirely disagree. I think I would've said Coldwell should be beaten with a stick or maybe a block of cheese, just for fun," I said.

"He's upset because someone broke into his house a few nights ago. They took some cash and left everything else. He's been a bit on edge because of course he's trying to work out the thing with the Governor's mansion and then someone broke into his house. We both know how Coldwell is so although I think it was probably just a stupid teenager, it has been on his mind," Jack explained.

I nodded, not entirely sure what to say. As Jack mentioned him thinking it was possibly a "stupid teenager" I thought of Amaris and her telling the boys to steal something for her. I wonder if one of them had been stupid enough to steal some cash from a random house that had turned out to belong to Jonas. On the other hand, it was entirely possible that it was Coldwell behind it. It would be exactly the type of thing he would do, some low-level harassment to scare Jonas.

We kept skating, me holding Jack's hand, and soon I let go of Coldwell possibly breaking into Jonas's house. I had a quiet, comforting moment right now and I decided to hold onto it.

CHAPTER SIXTEEN

"*D*o you have a plan for what you're going to do once the play closes?" Peta asked, starting up her car.

I got in the passenger seat and closed the door, gazing out at the protesters across the road in front of the theater who were now shouting and stomping around, seeming to get more angry with every passing day.

"Nope. I guess I could bite the bullet and work for Carter. It seems like there's plenty of news to report in town. How about you?"

Peta reversed and then we took off down the street, the sound of the protesters fading into the distance.

"I'm the same. I don't have a plan. It was good working at the cafe."

"You know, Molly and Luce do need help," I suggested.

"Maybe that then?" Peta said. "You can work too. Every café needs a hot waitress," she joked.

"A few shifts from my cousins, some from the moms, my diminishing part-time job at the library and I might be able to put together a basic minimum wage job out of it," I said, sounding far more gloomy than I meant to be.

"Are you still working on your story? The one with the ghost?"

"Sort of. I mean, I work on it when I have free time which at the moment is *never* so I guess I'm still *technically* working on it. It's probably been a couple of weeks now," I said.

I didn't want to tell Peta the truth which was that I felt pretty much like the ghost character in my story, floating around town, seeing life passing by.

I'm sorry, that sounds dark! It's just there had been a feeling building up inside of me over the days. I don't know, maybe connected to Aunt Ro and Sheriff Hardy getting married? Maybe it was connected to seeing Cool Blades turned into the Harlot Bay Ice Skating Rink and Entertainment Center. Everything was changing and it would continue to change, whether I wanted it to or not. I felt that I was being pulled along by events rather than driving them, a passenger in my own life.

Peta has always had the uncanny ability to virtually read my thoughts, being that she has been one of my closest friends my entire life.

"As soon as the play's over you can get back to writing that story, which I very much want to read. People were reading the *Harlot Bay Reader*, even though you were writing about foreshore restoration. I mean come on, you made foreshore restoration an exciting topic!" Peta said.

I laughed and yes, I did feel a little better.

We were on our way to the one and only costume shop in Harlot Bay, Black Cat Costumes, the place where a long, long time ago under the influence of being drugged I had apparently rented a sunflower costume and then worn it while running off into the streets of Harlot Bay. Peta and I had been sent to buy some spirit gum and other odds and ends that we needed as we reached the end of rehearsals and we'd soon move into the one week of production.

We were passing Aunt Cass's *Chili Challenge* office when I waved Peta over and asked her to stop for a moment.

"What's up?" Peta said once we parked.

"I want to ask Aunt Cass if we're anywhere on this salamander. I think I could handle life a bit better if I didn't have to keep going out at night down to those stormwater drains to collect water," I said.

"Let's go for it," Peta said.

I marched across the road with Peta following behind me. Although Aunt Cass had given us instructions to collect water and return the sample strips to her, the fact was we had barely seen her over the last few weeks. Partially that was me not going down to the main part of the mansion because the protesters were staying there still. There were no more family dinners running and at most we'd see Aunt Cass as a passing presence as we delivered the water testing strips and samples to her. She was busy at the *Chili Challenge* office most days, for once keeping out of trouble.

I went into the office without bothering to knock and saw that the large warehouse space was packed to the rafters with boxes of chili sauce, cowboy hats, stopwatches, and wet wipes. The last time I'd been here the place had been virtually empty as we'd nearly run out of chili sauces when Aunt Cass had been missing and frozen. It seemed she had made nice with all of her suppliers, paid them off and gotten the business back on its feet. I was expecting her teenage staff to be there, packing boxes, but there was no one in the warehouse. I could hear Aunt Cass out in the office humming to herself as she typed away on her laptop that now and then let out a witch cackle as she set off an email. I rapped on the office door and let myself in, Peta following behind me.

"What's up Peta, Peta pumpkin eater?" Aunt Cass said, standing up and holding out her hand for a high five.

"Uh not much Cassandra, Cassandra... I don't know what rhymes with Cassandra," Peta said and slapped her palm.

"How about you? Do you have a high five for your great aunt, your *very* great aunt?" Aunt Cass quipped.

I slapped her palm. The moment our hands touched there was a burst of noise so strong it knocked me off my feet.

There was a roaring so loud it sounded like a hurricane. I could hear three women chanting a spell of some kind. Then there was an echo, younger voices, chanting a spell but something went wrong. There was shouting and then sound of cracking as though the ice over a lake was too thin to walk on. I heard a man say "I will," and then the sound was gone, leaving me laying on my back, blinking up at Aunt Cass and Peta who had their hands outstretched to lift me up.

"I know I'm strong but I'm not *that* strong," Aunt Cass said. They lifted me up off the ground and then I sat down in the chair that was on the other side of Aunt Cass's desk.

"It's this slip power. I keep hearing all kinds of crazy noises and that one was really loud. People chanting, some man saying 'I will', people yelling something had gone wrong. I don't know," I said. Already it seemed sort of like a dream, the details quickly slipping.

"Is that what you came here for, just to touch me to see if you could hear something?" Aunt Cass said, sitting back behind her desk and returning to her laptop.

"Actually, no, I want to know what's going on with the salamander because I'm getting tired of going out late at night. I'm busy enough without having to go traipsing around grimy tunnels collecting water," I said, starting to get a little sarcastic.

"Okay, but we need to make this quick before my staff gets back from the coffee run," Aunt Cass said. She stood up, clapped her hands together, and I felt the magic surge. When she pulled them apart she was holding the map of the stormwater drains with all of the small testing strips stuck to it. She laid it out on the table in front of us.

"How did you do that?" I said.

"As always, if you want to learn you just have to ask. I can teach you but you need to be careful because if you try to summon something that's too big, you'll die," Aunt Cass said matter-of-factly.

"Oh, I can teach you but by the way, you'll *die*, yes, sounds real inviting," I said.

"So this is what you're using to track the salamander?" Peta said distracting both of us from what could become an argument.

Aunt Cass pointed to some of the strips. There were pink ones and then brown ones. There didn't seem to be any pattern that I could discern although there were slightly more pink ones on the edge of town nearest to our decaying mansion.

"Something is interfering with it. I'm getting odd readings all over the place. I'm not sure but maybe there's more than one salamander," Aunt Cass said.

I stood up and glared down at the map as though I could force it to reveal its secrets with an angry look.

"Well, whatever it is we need to do something. The teenagers in the play are going crazy. I think one of them, although I don't have any evidence about this, broke into someone's house just to steal money because a girl told him to because he believes he's in love. Those protesters who were all calm and easy-going are now yelling and stomping and I'm sure they're on the brink of punching somebody," I said.

"Oh I'm aware. Sheriff Hardy has already told me that there has been an increase in the number of assault cases and also break-ins across Harlot Bay," Aunt Cass said. We heard some voices outside, the three staff members returning from the coffee run. Aunt Cass folded the map and then there was a surge of magic and it disappeared between her hands.

Tabby, James and Even appeared outside the office, Tabby giving us a wave.

"Be with you in a second," Aunt Cass called out. She closed the door after taking her coffee.

"Look, I think I have a few other ideas about where the salamander might be. If you want to help me solve it, I'm going to need you to come rock climbing with me. I have some caves I need to check," Aunt Cass said.

"When you say caves you need to check, do you mean deep ones that are wet and probably scary?" I asked suspiciously.

"Of course, is there any other kind? So are you in? If you want your nights back you need to help me," she said.

"Sure, let's do it, why not. At least it's doing something," I said.

"That's the spirit. Well not really the spirit but good. We'll go after Ro's wedding. I've been thinking that *that's* a ceremony that might have a lot of emotion, so if we're very lucky, the salamander might be attracted. Hopefully I can set out some traps and catch it and we won't have to go into any caves at all," she said.

We said goodbye to Aunt Cass and her staff members and then went back out of the car to continue on our way to the costume shop.

"That looks like some progress. Go down to the caves, catch the salamander, no more having to go out at night. Or Aunt Cass catches it at the wedding. Everyone calms down. Those protesters stop yelling, random girls in the street stop scowling at me, and that crazy one who punched me never does anything like that again," Peta said. She touched her cheek where the bruise had been from the punch she'd taken not too long ago.

"It'd be good to catch it at the wedding because I don't want to go down to a cave," I said, starting to think I'd been too hasty in agreeing to do so.

We arrived at Black Cat Costumes and rushed inside. Peta grabbed all of the six bottles of spirit gum they had in stock. This was only meant to be a quick trip out to buy supplies but with the stop at Aunt Cass's we were taking far longer than we probably should. I got out the list and grabbed a few more things, including a feather boa that we needed for one particular scene that was a wild interpretation of the Bard's words.

The shop owner, Maurice, chatted away with us as we grabbed things off the list. Once we had it all we went to the cash register to pay for it.

"I'm glad the Mayor pulled some strings to arrange to bring this production to town. I've been selling so many supplies! It has been great for my business," he said.

"Well we're not done yet, so we'll probably be back. Are you going to order more spirit gum?" Peta asked.

"Yes, I have an entire case on back order. I can't believe that I've sold out. It just keeps flying off the shelves left and right," he said.

We grabbed our things and rushed back out to Peta's car, putting all the supplies on the back seat before driving away back to the theater.

"How much spirit gum are we using exactly? I know we have Anton's fake nose and Aunt Cass's makeup as Sly but are we seriously going through that much of it?" I asked, turning one of the spirit gum bottles over in my hand.

"I think we are. I just keep on buying bottles of it. I'm sure some of the teenagers are taking it for whatever stupid thing, wearing fake eyebrows or whatever, but yeah we're going through a huge amount of it. I hope that shipment comes in soon because we're going to need it through the production," Peta said.

We pulled up across the road from the theater and braced ourselves to rush through the protesters who were now shouting and stomping even louder than before.

"Don't worry, it'll all be over soon," Peta said to me with a wink.

"And then we can go be waitresses," I said and gave her smile in return.

CHAPTER SEVENTEEN

"Oh goddess, I can't find my bra!" Molly wailed, rushing around the lounge, looking for the bra that was, in fact, in her hand at that moment.

"You're holding it. You need to relax," I said, although I was feeling very far from relaxed myself.

"Oh right, I'll try this one on. These dresses aren't providing very much support," Molly said.

"Do you think we should wear shoes up to the wedding? There are a few stones between here and the forest," Luce said.

"I guess we could wear shoes, but then we're going to have to dump them somewhere," I said, adjusting my dress.

The wedding had crept up on us and then sprinted. It was heading past five o'clock, the sun going down, and the three of us were frantically trying to get ready. Aunt Ro had given us dresses, thin flimsy things that were utterly beautiful. The three of us looked like wild forest nymphs, which was good, especially given that we had garlands of wildflowers to wear in our hair.

The wedding was to take place up around behind the

Torrent mansion in the forest, and then the reception, if you could call it that, was nearby where there would be an enormous bonfire and tables of food. There would be non-witchy guests at the wedding, but obviously there were quite a lot of witchy elements. Jack, Will and Ollie hadn't arrived yet but had been given instructions by the moms what to wear: black pants, white shirts, no shoes. Aunt Ro and Sheriff Hardy's wedding was to be a wild wedding, one connecting with nature, and in deference to Aunt Ro being a kitchen witch, one that was to be followed by an enormously ridiculous amount of food. Even Adams was coming along, wearing his red bow tie and under strict instructions not to speak in front of anyone who wasn't a witch.

There was already a line of cars parked out front of the mansion, various police officers and Sheriff Hardy's family members and friends from around town. There were people making their way up behind the mansion, some of them wearing shoes, others barefoot, taking their shoes off when they got out of the car and walking gingerly across the gravel and up onto the grass that led up into the forest.

"I knew we should have had a bucket or something where people could put their shoes, like a shoe cloakroom," Luce said. Molly emerged from her room with a different bra in place.

"Oh no, no, no, no, no, you can't wear that one," Luce said.

"Why not? It looks good," Molly protested.

"Remember what you said, no more than a credit card worth of cleavage. That's like the national debt size of cleavage! Change it for something more demure," Luce instructed.

Molly returned to her bedroom grumbling to itself. She'd just emerged from her bedroom with a far more demure bra in place when the three boys arrived, all of them pulling their shoes off when they came inside and leaving them by the door. I must admit the three of them in their black pants and white shirts somewhat took our breath away, but I think we had a far more devastating effect on them.

"Oh wow," Will breathed, looking Luce up and down.

"You look like forest nymphs," Ollie said.

"You're beautiful," Jack breathed.

Those butterflies, the ones that flutter in your stomach, returned and I felt myself blushing. That was only for a moment though. The three of us then flung ourselves across the room and nearly tackled our respective boys to the ground. There was quite a lot of kissing until the front door opened and Aunt Cass came marching in, wearing an exquisite green dress the color of a rainforest.

"Alright lovers, let's go, we have a wedding," she instructed.

We gave ourselves one final adjustment, checked our boyfriends, and then all of us headed outside and up into the forest. One of the reasons we were slightly late was that Aunt Cass had pressed the three of us into service to help set up some magical traps out in the forest in the hope that the salamander might arrive, drawn by the emotions and love at the wedding. It had been a new spell, one that was quite simple really. Essentially, if the salamander walked over one of the traps it would freeze in place and we'd sense it. When that happened we'd only have about twenty minutes to collect it in a spelled cage that Aunt Cass had stashed behind a tree.

We made our way up into the forest following the pathway of glimmering lights in the trees. The sun was still going down so they weren't shining brightly yet, but when it grew dark they would be lighting up the night. We reached the large clearing where Sheriff Hardy was standing in bare feet, wearing his black pants and white shirt. He had his best man beside him, a friend who had traveled from out of town, called Eric. He was looking around at the assembled crowd with a smile on his face. We said goodbye to our men, giving them one last final kiss, and then rushed off to the small alcove in the forest where Aunt Ro and the moms were waiting. The moms were wearing similar dresses to us, looking more like nature witches than kitchen witches. Aunt Ro's wedding gown was a vivid green like jade, her hair studded with shining gems and intertwined with wildflowers.

"Mom, you look beautiful," Molly said, her voice thick.

"No one cries, we're all wearing too much mascara for there to be any crying," Aunt Cass said, even as she wiped away a tear. Aunt Ro gave the three of us each a kiss and then our moms adjusted our dresses as we tried to hold back our grumbling that they were already looking perfect.

Once we were all ready, Aunt Cass stepped forward and from a small pocket in her dress pulled out a glinting locket.

"This is April's, she wore it on her wedding day," Aunt Cass said.

We all stood still trying desperately not to cry and ruin our mascara as Aunt Cass fastened it around Aunt Ro's neck.

"April is here, I can feel it," Aunt Cass whispered.

That set off another round of seven witches trying not to cry. Finally we got ourselves together and then in the distance music started up, a violin playing a wedding tune.

"Okay time for you to get married. He's a good man," Aunt Cass said.

Me, Molly and Luce led the way, taking the role of flower girls essentially. Behind us came Mom and Aunt Freya, followed by Ro, and then at the rear, Aunt Cass.

We walked into the clearing. A hush went across the crowd. The sun was just going down and in the twilight the small gems in Aunt Ro's hair shimmered. Our dresses picked up glints of light as we walked, the diaphanous material faintly glowing. Although I was concentrating on walking, not crying, and smiling at everyone, I could still feel the magic. In some places it was calm and felt familiar. This was our land. This was our place. This is where our family had been for many years. It felt as though generations of Torrent witches were watching over us and keeping us safe. In other places I could feel the magic surge and push as though the emotions of everyone around us was pulling on it. I saw Jack standing over to the side looking across at me, his eyes wide, a dark blue in the dimming light. He stood beside his brother Jonas, and Peta who grinned at me and gave me a little wave. I gave her a wave back.

We walked up to the floral arch and took our place on one side of it. The moms came to stand beside us and then finally Aunt Cass after she gave Aunt Ro a kiss on the cheek. Because Grandma April was frozen down in the basement and her husband, Grandpa, who'd we'd never met, had died years ago there was no one to give Aunt Ro away, so Aunt Cass was standing in for that role.

You might think that at a somewhat witchy wedding, we'd have a somewhat witchy wedding celebrant, but we had a local woman by the name of Meredith from one of the churches that Sheriff Hardy had attended when he was a child and young man.

Sheriff Hardy and Aunt Ro came together and joined hands.

"My love," Sheriff Hardy murmured.

"My darling," Aunt Ro said in return.

The violin faded away and Meredith began the service: "Dearly beloved..."

Much like Hilda and Arlan's wedding, the part of it that made the marriage was quite short. In deference perhaps to the traditional, non-witchy side of the gathering, the wedding vows were the standard ones: in sickness and in health, and so on. The sun went down and the forest was lit up by lanterns casting a warm glow over everyone. Although the guests could not know it, there were also certain witchy spells in effect making sure any insects kept their distance. I couldn't tell exactly, but I think possibly Aunt Cass had cast some spell on the weather as well. I could feel something giant and powerful moving at a distance. I'm sure if I glanced down into Harlot Bay and found it was raining, it would not be raining up here on the hill with us.

Aunt Ro and Sheriff Hardy kissed and then there was an explosion of light high above us as fireworks shot up into the air, hidden out in the tree line. The crowd gasped and clapped and then the music struck up. Aunt Ro and Sheriff Hardy were laughing as they embraced Aunt Cass, Sheriff Hardy wagging his finger at her and then giving her an enormous kiss on the cheek.

There were huge tables of food off to the side that somehow amongst all the crazy wedding preparations the moms had made. Some people went for that, but most joined in the dancing, the wild sound of the violin taking hold of us. I grabbed Jack, kissed him and then danced on the grass, feeling surrounded by the warmth and love of family and friends, and the wild nature of the forest.

The night spun on in a blur. Too much wine, too much dancing, too much food, too much laughter. But as is the case with these things there can never be too much in moments like this. It was one of those moments where you became acutely aware of the passing of time, of the transitory nature of all things, that all of us dancing and laughing in the forest would one day be replaced by an entirely new group of people doing the same. We had to make our happiness, but we had to take it and hold onto it for the moment.

Eventually the night wound down, guests and friends kissing and hugging and waving goodbye. I walked down the hill holding Jack's hand, giddy from too much wine, my head and spirit spinning from too much dancing, too much happiness. Somewhere far behind, Sheriff Hardy and Aunt Ro

TESS LAKE

followed, coming down to fall into the back seat of Harlot Bay's one and only limousine that would then take them to a hotel in town where they were staying in a honeymoon suite.

I stumbled inside, heading for the warmth of my bed, pulling Jack along with me. I did not care one bit for the sorrows of the world at that moment. The night was perfect. But alas, like all things, such perfection was transitory. Many of Harlot Bay's police force had been at the wedding, but a few had been obliged to stay behind and they'd already been out on a call: a woman's body found dumped in the forest.

Olivia Knapp, the girl in love with Henry G, poisoned and abandoned to die.

CHAPTER EIGHTEEN

"*T*he show must go on! The show must go on!" Hans roared, his face red, apoplectic with rage.

"Someone died. You need to shut the show down," Sheriff Hardy repeated through gritted teeth.

"Art is the only defense against death," Hans yelled in Sheriff Hardy's face.

"If you yell at me again I'm going to arrest you," Sheriff Hardy said, his face beginning to turn red.

"For what? Fighting against death with art the only way I know how?" Hans proclaimed, looking as though he was saying lines that he would put in his next autobiography.

"No, it's for being an ass," Sheriff Hardy said.

I was standing by the stage with Peta on one side and Marcus Fyfe on the other. It was the day after Sheriff Hardy's wedding and the news had spread across town that a woman had been found dead in the forest. Tonight was opening night and we were meant to gather for one last run through before we opened in the evening. But everything was ruined, a disaster. Olivia was gone, dead, found foaming at the mouth. It was easy to see she'd been poisoned by whoever had poisoned Hans. Again, a venomous snake was suspected given the snake that had been let loose in the theater, which had eventually been confirmed as an Australian tiger snake.

Now the police were trying to put together Olivia's last movements to find out where she had been last night.

Given her death, Sheriff Hardy wanted to shut the play down, but Hans was fighting him, realizing ultimately the Sheriff didn't have the power to stop the play going ahead.

I looked away from Hans who was still red-faced but managed to lower his voice as he was talking with Sheriff Hardy. I could feel my stomach churning, a kind of sick hollow feeling that no amount of food could get rid of. I'd already talked with Jack and he had wanted me to stop as well, said that he'd pull the fire alarm himself if that's what it took to shut the play down. Part of me agreed with him. It was clear that whomever poisoned Hans was doing their best to stop the play. Their attempted murder had now become actual murder. But the other half of me shared the sentiment the teenagers and everyone else in the play did: *the show must go on*. Everyone had worked so hard under such horrible conditions struggling, rehearsing over and over for hours, even in the face of danger and sabotage. They didn't want to stop, for it all to have been for nothing. Even though I wasn't going on stage, I felt the same way. Perhaps if we could just get through our opening night, increase the number of guards looming around the place, things would be okay. Jack had grudgingly accepted my position, although honestly I wasn't too sure of it myself.

As Sheriff Hardy and Hans continued to talk and everyone stood around mute and shocked, I noticed there was something stuck to my shoe. I knelt down and peeled it off. It was a perfectly arched eyebrow, probably lost at some stage during the play. It was sticky with spirit gum on the back of it. I squished it in half and then stuffed it in my pocket so I could throw it away later.

"Did you see Henry G? Does he know yet?" I asked Marcus in an undertone.

"I have no idea if he knows," Marcus whispered back.

"Aren't you guys all staying at the same house?"

"Nope, it's in his contract, he has his own place," Marcus said and then quickly quieted when Hans shot a glare in our direction.

Quite a while ago, Hollywood movie people had come to town to shoot a film. Having more money than sense they'd rented empty houses all over Harlot Bay with virtually one person from the production to a house. Hans's theater company didn't have as much money so it had rented entire houses, the big ones that had lots of rooms and then the lighting assistants and various people working on the production got a room to themselves. I just assumed that Henry G was staying at the same place as Marcus Fyfe and some of the other men.

Sheriff Hardy finally departed. His men had spent the morning searching the entire theater from top to bottom, looking for anything dangerous, any sign of sabotage, but hadn't found anything. As soon as they were gone, Hans roared out again: "Back to rehearsal, from the top, start again," he yelled.

Despite the terror of the day we all moved, operating like a well-oiled machine. The former director Emilion had taught as well, but now he was gone, replaced by Hans. We didn't even see him to say goodbye. We'd just arrived for rehearsal and there was Hans, looking fit and well for a man who'd been poisoned and touched the very face of death.

The play began and soon Aunt Cass was up in the role of the drunken Tinker, Christopher Sly. She was halfway through a line when Hans shouted out "Stop! That's terrible, do it again."

Aunt Cass, to her credit, did the line again but again he yelled out to stop.

"That's the worst acting I have ever seen. Do it again!" She repeated the line and again he shouted, again and again. Five times we went through the loop of Aunt Cass saying the same line. Out of everything that could have scared me it was the look on Aunt Cass's face that was the worst. After he had shouted for the fifth time, she stomped her foot on the stage and I swear in the distance I heard thunder rumbling.

"Give me some direction then. Don't just say *do it again*. What you want me to do?" Aunt Cass said. Her voice was dark and cold and if Hans had known what she really was he would have been quaking in his boots.

Hans stood up from his chair and walked closer to the stage. "What I want you to do is audition for my next play. We're going to be putting on *Macbeth* and I think there's a role for you. Here's the line that you can practice: 'Double, double, toil and trouble, fire burn and cauldron bubble.' It'll be perfect for an old witch like you!" Hans shouted.

The look on Aunt Cass's face would have killed a lesser man. I cringed, feeling sure that there'd be a flash of light and then just a grease stain on the ground where Hans had stood. I knew he'd just been insulting her as he'd been insulting everyone all morning but the witch comment hit far too close to home.

Aunt Cass frowned at him and then gave him a gentle smile before adjusting her clothing and delivering the line again.

Hans didn't shout out this time but rather glared at her and then walked back to his chair to continue watching the play. It felt like there had been a battle of wills, but because she hadn't fought him she had possibly won somehow.

We sped through the play, Hans occasionally bursting into a rage, the teenagers scampering about, the feeling of fear and terror but somehow out of that came incredible performances. The words came alive. Kira was Katherine the shrew; Amaris was Bianca, her sister; Anton was their father decreeing that the younger can only wed when the elder one did.

There were betrayals and mistakes, people pretending to be others, dressing up. The play flowed through the auction and then to the final scene where Kira delivered her speech about obeying one's husband.

The doors of the theater were closed, but outside I could still faintly hear the protesters chanting. It seemed an appropriate backdrop to that final speech which was probably the most controversial of the entire play, the one which people argued over the most. Was Katherine, the tame shrew, now *truly* tamed by her husband and the obedient wife? Or was she giving the speech, presenting one face in public, but being different in private, knowing that to advance her husband's power was to advance her own?

Whatever the answer, Kira gave a masterful performance of it.

We finished up the play. Hans merely grunted "Good" and then walked off to his dressing room.

We cleaned up and reset for tonight, and then Aunt Cass found me.

"I have a lead on where the salamander is. Come on, we need to go," she said.

CHAPTER NINETEEN

"*I*'m impressed you didn't turn Hans into a grease spot," I said to Aunt Cass as we drove back to the mansion.

"I think that man is going to get what's coming to him," she said cryptically.

"You think someone is going to murder him, don't you?"

Aunt Cass looked out the window out over Harlot Bay as we drove up the hill.

"No, I don't think so but I believe he's going to be ruined. That's what my intuition tells me."

"Is that why you smiled when he was shouting at you?"

"Oh that? No, I just had a sudden idea about where the salamander might be. We'll grab the climbing gear and go behind the mansion," she said.

Aunt Cass refused to elaborate on exactly where we were going so eventually I gave up and drove until we got home. She ducked inside, grabbed the climbing gear which she forced me to carry, and then I followed her up around behind the mansion, into the forest. There is plenty of land up behind the mansion. Lots of space with the cottages and things other witches had built and abandoned. On one side it slopes down, eventually joining farmland, and on the other it is a cliff with some very rickety old wooden stairs and others carved into the rock.

We stopped near a small opening in the ground, which I knew led down into some caves. When we were children we had been warned never to go into them, and considering they were scary and dark we had eagerly obeyed that instruction. Aunt Cass put her climbing harness on and then helped me buckle mine up.

"Is this going to be safe?" I asked, really not wanting to go down into the dark and scary cave.

"You're with me, of course it's not safe," Aunt Cass said with a devilish grin. She tied the climbing rope around a thick tree and then connected an electric winch to the line, which she then connected to us.

"If we get stuck we just hit the button, it'll pull us right back up," she said.

"Okay, I guess," I said.

Aunt Cass went first, edging down into the hole, letting out rope as she went. I followed behind her partially because, well, if my eightyish-year-old great aunt could do it then I should be able to as well. As soon as we were underground we both cast floating lights to illuminate the area around us. It was wet and damp but didn't smell unpleasant, like the stormwater drains. It just smelt of dirt and stone. We climbed down a ledge and then Aunt Cass used the winch to lower us down another ten feet or so until we found another level of the cave. It opened into a small area where there was black moss growing. Below us was another hole that descended into inky darkness.

"Do you feel that?" Aunt Cass whispered.

I closed my eyes and tried to relax, which was extremely hard, considering the circumstances. The magic this far down was still, like a pond that had been untouched. But yes, there it was, some warm edge, something that shouldn't be there. It was radiating out from somewhere below us.

"What is that? Is that the salamander?"

"I don't think it is, but I believe that it's part of the puzzle," Aunt Cass said.

We let our lights float down below us and Aunt Cass hit the winch to lower us down gently. We descended into the dark and quiet, the only sounds the winch, our breathing, and distant dripping water.

The air temperature dropped as we descended. The light only illuminated a small space around us but I could feel that we had lowered into a much larger area, the cave expanding into the distance. We brightened the floating lights but even then they could not illuminate the entire cave system which stretched off into the distance.

"Oh goddess we're so far up," I whispered, trying not to look down at the drop.

"Or we're so far *down* would be another way to look at it," Aunt Cass said and then laughed.

Eventually, we reached the ground and Aunt Cass unhooked us. There was no natural light in any direction, just black, the only illumination the glowing orbs that we had summoned. Now that we were here, I could feel whatever it was, the radiating force. Aunt Cass pointed in a direction and I nodded. We began clambering over rocks, watching out for small pools of water, hearing dripping and also in the distance the sound of a gently burbling stream. As we moved, the sensation of something radiating at us became stronger. I couldn't help but think of Jack, him appearing in my mind, and Aunt Ro's wedding. I imagined it was him standing by the altar, me wearing the green wedding dress, walking up and clasping his hand. Then we'd kiss and be married and dance away under the stars.

"Do you think Art is a good man?" Aunt Cass asked me in a distant voice.

"I think he might be. He seems to like you," I said. Aunt Cass obviously had her man on her mind as well.

We continued moving, clambering around a large boulder and then there in front of us was a pool, glimmering with pink sparkles of light. It was the source of the stream that we could hear burbling, running its way out of the cavern.

Aunt Cass pushed her light over above the pool and there, standing above it, were the wreckage of broken barrels, bright pink liquid dripping out of them into the basin below.

"The earthquake from the explosion must've done it. Shattered the barrels and set the love potion free," Aunt Cass said.

I made my way around the pool, careful not come too close. The barrels looked old and there had to be at least twenty of them. Maybe only four or five had broken.

"These are stamped with *The Merchant Arms*. That was the place Juliet Stern owned," I said.

"The girl must have been making a lot of love potion," Aunt Cass said.

"There must be a hundred gallons here. What if this floods the town?"

"A whole lotta love is what."

"Are you taking this seriously?"

Aunt Cass turned to me and gave me a sharp look.

"Would you prefer the unvarnished truth? If it floods out, people will die. There will be murders and violence. Love is not to be messed with - it is the most dangerous of all emotions. A person will kill in hatred but love? They'll burn the world."

"Okay, sorry! No need to get too melodramatic about it."

"Or perhaps you'd like me to talk about all the relation-ships currently running only because they had a little boost from the love potion in the water? We take this away and there is an almighty hangover coming. People are going to wake up in beds next to people they *definitely* don't love. Many will wish they could take back their… engagements."

"Are you talking about Will and Luce? No, he loves her! It was ages ago he messaged her about ring sizes."

"These barrels were broken when I fought that monster out on Truer Island. That's all I know."

"Seems like you're saying it's not true love."

"Who can know such things?" Aunt Cass said and turned away from me.

The cave was cold and I shivered. I had a sudden image of Jack bringing me cookies. Was that him or the love potion?

"Come over here and help me counter what has leaked out," Aunt Cass said.

I obeyed, my mind on other matters.

"We'll just do the potion that has leaked. I'll figure out what to do with the rest of the barrels later. Once it's gone we should have a better chance of finding that salamander."

We held hands and I followed Aunt Cass's lead.

The magic to counter is simple - flow of magic and a word.

As usual, I was soothed by the magic. The warmth of it, the patterns in the flow. We gathered it up and then let it out, directing it into the pool. There was an initial resistance, like pushing at a heavy box that didn't want to move. But after a moment, the counter broke through. The pool changed from sparkly pink to muddy brown. The color crept up the side of the bank and into the broken barrels, destroying the last of the escaped potion.

We held the spell for a good twenty minutes, letting it soak into the ground, reverting the potion. I could feel it draining on me but with Aunt Cass's help I managed to keep going until she called us to a halt.

She let go of my hands and looked around.

"There's still a hangover coming and there might be a tiny leak for a few weeks but I think we got most of it. Come on, let's go."

I followed Aunt Cass back to our ropes and the distant hint of light far above.

"How do I know whether Jack made cookies because he loves me or because of the potion?"

Aunt Cass hooked the rope to her gear and did the same for me, buckling me in.

"Has he ever made anyone else cookies?"

"I have no idea. Let's say no."

"Well then it's true love," she said.

"*So helpful.* Not flippant at all," I snapped.

I let my hovering light wink out. Only Aunt Cass's remained. It barely illuminated her face.

She sighed and the dark crept in closer.

"True love is easy to know. It's better than anything you've ever experienced and an agony when it's ripped away. It is a persistent voice telling you that all is right in the world. It is an aching loss."

She hit the button on the electric winch and we jerked up off the floor. We ascended, the tiny wisp of light below us fading away, leaving behind only a dark black pool.

I couldn't help but feel Aunt Cass was talking from personal experience.

CHAPTER TWENTY

$\mathscr{I}$t was chaos outside the theater. Hans being poisoned hadn't drawn any media at all despite his level of fame, but Olivia being found dead certainly had. Media from all across the country had descended on Harlot Bay and had immediately been attracted to the protesters outside the theater like flies to rotting meat. They then got exactly what they wanted when the protesters, who had been growing increasingly angry throughout the week, had finally lost their temper and one of them had hit a private security guard with their sign. The private security fought back and the media got a lot of footage of a violent altercation out the front of the theater. Then Sheriff Hardy had come, arrested half the protesters and half the private guards, and had them taken away. Now there were still protesters out the front but they were behind a line that Sheriff Hardy had drawn on the ground in chalk. The private security guards were on the other side, glaring at them, and all around were media making their solemn reports about how *the small town of Harlot Bay is once again the scene of tragedy.*

Inside the theater it was certainly no better. We were sold

out, the crowd murmuring excitedly. Behind the scenes it was chaos. Aunt Cass was missing, we were due to start in less than fifteen minutes, and she still hadn't put her makeup and costume on. Everyone was rushing everywhere like headless chickens. I was desperately trying to corral teenagers, stop some from crying, calming down Anton who was sweating so much his oversized prop nose kept coming unstuck, and also trying to keep myself calm and not run immediately to the fire alarm, hit it and then say everyone had to evacuate the building.

I was checking the racks of costumes by the side of the stage when someone tapped me on the shoulder. I whirled around, my heart in my throat, but then relaxed when I saw it was only Jack, Molly and Luce.

"Hey, came to say good luck and, you know if anything happens, let me know. I'll just be out there," Jack said.

"Okay, thanks," I said, still somewhat out of breath and not really listening.

"Yes, good luck," Molly said.

"Same here," Luce said. They were looking around, distracted, not paying any attention.

"Are you guys looking for something?" I asked.

"Is Aunt Cass around?" Molly asked.

I was about to say no, but as though she'd been summoned by the sound of her name, Aunt Cass appeared. In her arms was the mesh cage that she had constructed and in the bottom was a small pink lizard no larger than the palm of my hand.

"I got it! I knew as soon as that love potion was gone out of the water I'd be able to track it down," she said. She was grinning at the four of us who were standing there somewhat stunned.

"What? Where was the salamander?" I finally said.

"It was under the theater. It had set up a nest there. It

must've been all the teenagers with all their hormones and love and adventure and excitement and anger and fury and everything that's been going on here. Of course it would be drawn here! I found one of those trapdoors and went down there and it was amongst all that rubbish that someone's been dumping, all those spirit gum bottles and whatever," Aunt Cass said.

"Spirit gum?" Luce asked.

"Yeah you know, for costumes, makeup, that type of thing. There's enough down there that we could put a costume on everybody," Aunt Cass said.

"There's magic in the mayonnaise of the *Magic Bean* sandwiches," Molly blurted out to Aunt Cass.

"What? How do you figure that?" Aunt Cass asked.

"It's easy, we used one of those testing strips you gave us. It went pink straight away. They're using magic in their sandwiches. We hardly had any customers today. They're going to ruin us and they're using magic, some witch is doing it," Molly complained.

Aunt Cass shook her head.

"Or the strips also detect *tarragon*, which is probably what it found," she said. "Here, take this out and lock it in your car. I've sealed its magic away so its effect should start to recede fairly soon. Just make sure it doesn't escape," she said, thrusting the cage on Molly and Luce.

Henry G appeared, grabbed Aunt Cass by the arm and dragged her off to the dressing room to put her into makeup.

"Oh, *tarragon*," Luce said.

"Damn," Molly said.

They walked off with the salamander between them, leaving Jack and me alone.

"I have no idea what that's about, but if I was to guess, possibly there was a break-in at the *Magic Bean*?" Jack said.

"I have no comment, but possibly yes," I said, realizing

that although I had intended to tell Jack, it must have slipped my mind.

Jack gave me a quick kiss and then looked at me seriously. "If you see anything suspicious, hit that fire alarm, get people out of here. Sheriff Hardy sent a sample of Olivia's blood to a friend of mine who works in toxicology. They're putting a rush on it. There's someone around here doing something dangerous with poisons and we can't have any more deaths," he said.

I gave him a kiss and then he went back out the front to find his seat. Everything was moving too fast for me to worry about what someone with murderous intentions might do. Somewhere on the other side of the stage Hans was shouting at the top of his lungs, probably at some scared teenager. I saw Henry G rushing around in the dark getting costumes ready, and then one of the production assistants lowered the house lights. We were down to our three-minute warning, about to get started.

It seemed we went from chaos to calm in a minute flat. All the costumes were in place, the teenagers were ready, even Aunt Cass appeared dressed in her full makeup looking like the drunken old Tinker. Marcus started playing the piano and then we were away.

We were halfway through the first act when a ghost appeared right in front of me and I stifled a scream. It was Olivia. She saw me and she knew that I'd seen her.

"You can see me! Why is everyone else ignoring me?" she asked, her voice ethereal and haunting.

I moved away from the side of the stage so I couldn't be heard.

"You're dead Olivia, they found your body," I stammered trying to keep my voice low. Normally I'd be much more sensitive with a ghost but I was too shocked by seeing her appear.

"No, I'm not dead," she said and frowned.

"Where did you go yesterday? Did you visit anyone?" I asked. Olivia turned around and looked across backstage. There in the distance was Henry G. He was doing something with the prop swords.

"I thought he loved me," she whispered and began to move across the stage towards him. I saw Henry G grab a prop sword and rush off into the darkness in the direction of the dressing rooms.

I got a sudden sick feeling in the pit of my stomach.

I rushed off, sprinting through the dark behind the stage as fast as possible. I crashed into a teenager, someone I didn't recognize in their costume and heard of a burst of noise. It sounded like a horse right by my ear neighing. I pulled the stunned teenager up off the ground and walked into the darkness. In my pocket, my phone buzzed and for some reason I pulled it out although I had a fear running in the back of my mind that if Hans saw me with a phone out during a performance he would kill me. It was a message from Jack.

'Harlow, it's a frog toxin. Whoever killed Olivia owns frogs and probably snakes.'

In a blur, I typed my message in return.

'Come to the dressing rooms, bring Sheriff Hardy.'

I felt that awful twisting intuition again. The prickles up my spine. There had been guards everywhere, looming about the place but after the ones out the front had been arrested they were now more widely dispersed. I ran down the corridor until I reached Hans's dressing room. I shoved open the door only to find Hans alone, sitting at his desk with his arms crossed and a sour look on his face.

"What are you doing here?" he demanded.

I quickly checked the room but he was the only one in it.

Wherever Henry G had gone it wasn't here, if indeed it had been him who was up to something.

I couldn't see where Olivia's ghost had gone either.

"You're in danger. I think someone is going to poison you," I gasped.

"It's the stage. It has to be dangerous!" Hans proclaimed.

"No, you're really in danger, someone's going to –" I saw the copy of Hans's autobiography sitting on his desk and remembered a page showing a photo thirty years ago where people had given themselves absurd professions. I lunged over to the desk and opened it to the picture. There it was, Hans as chief snackologist, beside him Viola MacBeth as junior assistant to the junior *herpetologist*.

"Who is she to you? Who is Viola MacBeth? A herpetologist has to do with snakes right?" I said, pointing at the book with a shaking finger.

"Viola MacBeth? No one. I mean that quite literally. She's gone. She's nothing. She was nothing then and she is nothing now," Hans said, venom in his tone.

"Though this be madness, yet there is method in it," Henry G said as he stepped out of the dark.

I whirled around, standing between the two men.

Henry G had apparently appeared from nowhere. In his left hand he held the prop sword that was looking decidedly sharp. In his right he had a gun and it was pointed directly at Hans.

"You're not going to do anything," Hans sneered.

Henry G frowned at Hans, lifted the gun and pointed it at his head.

Olivia floated into the room.

"But I loved you, why did you kill me?" she said to Henry G. She drifted by me and I felt her cold fingers touch my shoulder.

I heard a faint echo of frogs croaking, a snake hissing.

"What are you doing with that gun Henry?" Hans sneered. Henry G leaned the sword against the wall, reached up and grabbed his face… and tore it away. Strands of rubbery material stretched and snapped, his face peeled off, along with his hair. Underneath was a woman, her hair cut short, an aged version of the face that was peering out from the photo in Hans's autobiography.

She picked up the sword again.

"When sorrows come, they come not single spies, but in battalions," she said.

"You're not going to do anything *Mary*, you never could," Hans sneered.

Henry G or Viola or Mary or whatever her name was, lifted the gun.

"Use my real name or you'll die," she said, gritting her teeth.

Hans looked afraid for a moment but then returned to his calculated sneering front.

"Very well, *Viola MacBeth*. I care not what you call yourself, a pile of garbage by any other name would smell as bad."

"Henry G was a woman? What?" Olivia said. I was the only one who could hear her.

"You don't have to do this Viola. I know that he hurt you," I said, desperately stalling for time and guessing what Hans had done to her.

Viola looked at me and peeled away the last remnants of the Henry G mask over her face. Her left ear was a ruin of scar tissue from old burns.

"He did more than hurt me. He ruined my reputation when he killed those people. His sabotage destroyed me. He made me into nothing and now I'm going to do the same to him," she said.

"You're still telling that lie Viola?" Hans said, mocking her.

Viola slipped the gun into her pocket and brought the sword to bear.

"I am merely going to do to you what you did to me. I hope you enjoy it," she said. She lunged, so quick, the sword passing by me by a whisper. It pricked Hans in the shoulder. He leaped up from his chair, shoved into me and I crashed against the door, falling to the floor. They wrestled, Hans getting the sword off her and Viola getting cut across the hand.

Whatever poison Viola had put on it was fast-acting because before I could get up off my feet she had collapsed and so had Hans.

I ran over to them.

"Under the theater somewhere there will be a bomb," Hans whispered.

"Why would she do that?"

"Because I did it to her," Hans said before passing out.

I stood up and turned towards Olivia who was floating in the darkness where Henry G, or Viola, had emerged. There on the floor was an open trapdoor, a hidden one that she had climbed from.

I was almost at it when the door to the dressing room crashed open and Jack came pelting in.

"Harlow!" he called out.

"Tell Sheriff Hardy there's a bomb! Get everyone out," I said and jumped down into the darkness.

I heard Jack shout something, probably at Sheriff Hardy who was likely right behind him. I landed at the bottom of a ladder in the pitch darkness. I quickly summoned a light revealing that I was in a set of rooms and corridors underneath the theater. I barely had a moment to look around before Jack came down the hole and landed beside me.

"We have to get out of here, Harlow! We need to get everyone out," he yelled.

"No, there's a bomb. If we can find it, I can stop it," I said.

I had no idea, of course, whether I could but I was too frantic, too crazed to think about it. I'd run to find it and then... do anything I could to stop it exploding.

We rushed away from the ladder, Jack tripping over a black garbage bag. It tore open and scattered empty spirit gum bottles everywhere. He got to his feet and we continued to run, looking around for a bomb. It was then, there in the distance that I saw a small blinking red light. We bolted towards it, passing a table filled with wigs on stands, a complete dressing table underground. I had the barest moment to realize this had been where Viola had been becoming Henry G every day. *She* had been the one using all the spirit gum to keep her costume together.

Oh Goddess, we had her over for dinner! She'd fooled us completely.

We skidded to a stop near the bomb. It didn't look like anything I'd seen on television. There was a small, blinking red light and then some dull gray blocks with black wires running to another black box.

"Is there anything magical you can do to stop it? Can you freeze it or pull it to pieces without it exploding?" Jack asked.

Now that I was standing in front of the bomb I had no idea what I could do. If Aunt Cass had taught me the spell to teleport things perhaps I could have moved it from here to somewhere out over the sea where it could explode harmlessly, but I didn't know how to do that.

"We need to get it away from here or we need to run," Jack urged.

"There's a stormwater drain near here. We could get rid of it there," I said, remembering the map I'd studied countless times. It was somewhere near the rear of the theater.

Without thinking I ripped the bomb off the wall, seeing

Jack flinch as I did. It didn't detonate so we didn't die, so I guess it was okay.

We ran through the gloom, the light bobbing along beside us. Soon we came to a room with WATER/UTILITY printed on the door. Inside it was dark and dank, an open manhole in the center of the floor.

I quickly climbed down, clutching the bomb to my chest. As soon as my feet hit the wet concrete I was off, my miniature sun lighting the way. Jack was mere footsteps behind me and then caught up, running alongside as we pelted through the darkness. We ran maybe a street underground and then I saw an edge, one of the stormwater drains descending into the dark. I threw the bomb and it disappeared, the red blinking light fading as it went.

"Come on!" Jack yelled and grabbed my hand. He'd meant to pull me back in the other direction away from the black darkness below, but then there was an enormous roar, a crack that sounded as though the earth itself had split in two, and then it seemed that darkness rushed up to consume us both.

CHAPTER TWENTY-ONE

"All I'm saying is, as a modern woman playing Katherine, is that I don't think it matters whether Shakespeare was super intelligent for his time and Katherine's speech at the end is all about her obeying her husband but secretly in private she has the power, or whether he was really a man of his time, and perhaps it was just a little bit sexist. Doesn't matter. The art tells a story and it compels us to think for ourselves, to contrast the way it was *then* and the way it is *now*. Besides do you see me obeying a man? I don't think so," Kira said and gave me a grin.

I pulled on my pants, feeling my body still aching from two days in the hospital.

"I think Katherine was being smart. Like you know when you say *I can't open the jar of pickles* and then you get him to do it and then he feels really good?" I said.

"Oh yeah or when you say can you get that book off that high shelf and it's not really *that* high and then he does and then your fingers touch and then *complications ensue* and then he becomes your boyfriend," Kira said in a rush. There were some footsteps outside my hospital door and then Fox appeared, returning with the coffee Kira had asked him to fetch.

"There he is. Okay, Harlow, stay strong H-bomb, whoops bomb, sorry," Kira said. Fox waved goodbye to me and then Kira grabbed his arm and pulled him out of the room.

It was two days since the bomb had detonated, two days since I had awoken with my ears ringing in the back of an ambulance, looked across and seen Jack covered in blood staring back at me. Both of us had appeared far worse than it was. Superficial wounds from the explosion and bits of concrete that had hit us. We'd both been kept in for observation. Jack was down the corridor from me and today we'd be going home. There had been a constant stream of visitors since I'd awoken. The moms and cousins and Aunt Cass at first obviously, fussing around me and then Jack down in his room, and then Sheriff Hardy. Incredibly they'd managed to get Viola - real name Mary - and also Hans to the hospital and save their lives despite the fact both of them had been poisoned with an exotic frog toxin.

Viola had almost died but Hans had survived perhaps because he had just recently been poisoned with the same toxin and had built up some resistance. I told Sheriff Hardy the full story, everything Viola had said, that she was merely doing to Hans what he had done to her, and then how Hans had said there must've been a bomb underneath the building. Sheriff Hardy had taken all that information away and then returned a day later telling me that, in fact, thirty years ago there had been an explosion at a theater where Hans and Viola had been working. Viola had been directing a play, *Much Ado About Nothing*, and something had exploded under the theater. People had died and ultimately she'd received the blame. They'd had a gas tank that was to belch out a burst of flame at a pivotal moment, in a wild interpretation of the play. The official report said that it exploded because safety protocols had not been adhered to.

With Hans leaping straight to there being a bomb underneath the theater it appeared he had made a confession of sorts and that investigation would be reopened.

Viola had awoken raving mad at Hans but also genuinely confused about what she had done. Sheriff Hardy had told me that she couldn't understand why she'd set the bomb that she'd known would have killed all the people inside the theater. He said that she initially only intended to poison Hans, to kill him, and that was all. The motivation for it was the autobiography and the cruel things he had written about her, how she'd been nothing to him. She'd always suspected that he'd sabotaged the gas bottle and caused the explosion, but after having her career ruined she had vanished, content to leave that pain in the past until Hans's autobiography had come out and smashed her into the ground once more. It was then that she had donned the guise of Henry G, making herself up as an expert costumer and joining Hans to work for him to look for her moment to exact her revenge.

Sheriff Hardy had known about the salamander. We of course had told him and it was my belief that the influence of it had magnified her emotions and perhaps even led her to take her extreme course of action. Sadly, it was all something that we had to keep secret. The facts of the case, if you took the magic out of it, were that someone set a bomb under a crowded theater and that hundreds of people were very lucky not to be dead. It ultimately didn't matter whether magic had influenced her. The law would move its course and she would go to prison, Hans probably closely behind her.

Sheriff Hardy and his men had searched Viola's rented house and found numerous glass terrariums full of frogs and snakes. Viola had been feeding the frogs a particular diet to make them poisonous. She'd then used this to poison Hans, and later, Olivia.

Poor Olivia... I hadn't seen her ghost since I jumped down the secret trapdoor. The salamander had affected her, causing her to fall in love with Henry G. They had found her diary, including an entry where she had decided to go to his house to declare her love for him.

Viola wasn't speaking about it so we could only assume Olivia had discovered the frogs and snakes and Viola had poisoned her to stop her revealing her secrets.

It was a horrible mess. The salamander was just an animal, albeit a magical one. There was no malice or intent behind it. It just *was*... and from that, Olivia had ultimately died. It was again a serious reminder: magic was not to be trifled with or underestimated.

There were still threads not tied off. Who were the strange people filming the theater who were clearly wearing disguises? I didn't know and honestly, after being almost blown up, I didn't care. I had enough other things on my mind. The papers going missing from the Library. Hattie appearing younger than she apparently was (I was having trouble keeping that in my mind). Coldwell and the Mall.

Change had also come to the Torrent Mansion. Aunt Ro had moved out to live with Sheriff Hardy. I hadn't been home yet so I didn't know *what* that would be like.

That reminded me: the moms, Aunt Cass and their respective lover boys. Me, Molly and Luce hadn't forgotten about them but in the rush of everything hadn't had the opportunity to fully drag them all over the hot coals, as they had so often done to us. It was going to be *fun.*

I was checking my things when I heard a knock on the door.

"Come in," I said. It was Marcus, the music director.

"Good to see you up and moving," he said and gave me a smile.

"It was a lot of luck is all," I said.

Marcus stood there for a moment and then cleared his throat. He looked down at his feet.

"I'm sorry I didn't tell anyone earlier. I mean, I suspected that Henry G was someone in costume. I didn't care that Hans was poisoned and no one really got injured by the sandbags, and I guess by the time the snake turned up I thought it was just ridiculous rather than incredibly deadly. I don't know, I was playing detective. I smuggled in the water balloons to dump on Henry G because I thought he was wearing a costume and if I could get him wet it would reveal it. That obviously didn't work," he mumbled.

"He's caught now - or, she is. I suppose sometimes it's best to let the police handle these things," I said, feeling like the largest hypocrite in the world.

"Did you hear the kids have been putting the play on in the park?" Marcus said, changing the topic.

"Kira tells me it's been sold out, although there are no tickets," I said.

"It's amazing. I've been playing on the electric keyboard connected to an amp system. It is an incredible performance," Marcus said.

When Jack appeared in the doorway, Marcus said hello and goodbye all in one moment and then left. Jack was covered in tiny cuts on his face and neck. There were also some on his body that you couldn't see under his shirt. I certainly didn't look any better.

Jack hugged me and looked down at his shoe, which was untied. He knelt down and did it up, again bending on one knee in front of me. Then he looked up and took my hand. "Harlow Torrent, will you…"

"You gotta stop this joke buddy, or you're going to be thankful that you're in a hospital," I said laughing.

"Will you help me up off the floor?" Jack teased. I pulled him up and then squeezed him close, although not too hard because both of us were still a little sore.

We headed out of the hospital, going out a back exit to avoid any media that might still be hanging around. Molly and Luce had told me that Carter had run wild in his paper spinning up all kinds of conspiracy theories and the truth was that the reality was probably crazier than his conspiracies. Someone from thirty years ago came to get revenge and then almost succeeded in their plan.

We were driving back to the mansion in Jack's truck when he looked over at me and said "You have a secret lair, don't you?"

It was such a surprising question that I laughed and then quieted down.

"Yes, actually I do, it's in a cottage up behind the mansion," I said.

"I figured as much," he said. We drove in silence for a bit and eventually we reached the mansion, parking at our end of it. The family had all come and gone at the hospital and they were now back at work. Molly and Luce were at *Traveler* handling the coffee side of business. They had told me on a visit they weren't cut out for the cafe lifestyle and so Peta was going to take the cafe over, rename it, and they were going to run it still with the businesses connected. Peta had given me an open offer to take a job with her too. The three of them were still on the hunt for a guitarist with *just* the right amount of scruffiness.

The moms were back at work at the bakery and Aunt Cass had returned to the *Chili Challenge*. The protesters had left after the opening night of the *Taming of the Shrew* had been shut down, apparently choosing not to care if a bunch of teenagers were putting on the same play in a park. So it was just Jack and me when we got back to the mansion. We walked inside to find Adams on the sofa watching television and beside him, a beautiful blonde cat with vivid green eyes. She was wearing a diamante collar that looked very familiar.

"Oh, hey, Adams, who is this?" I asked.

"I'm Butterscotch," the blonde cat said and then blinked her green eyes at me.

Jack and I stood there for a moment in stunned silence before finally he spoke. "Two talking cats, awesome, wow," he said.

"Let's get out of here," I said, feeling like I had intruded on a date. We dropped our bags and I grabbed Jack's hand, and we exited out the door, making our way around the side of the mansion and up towards the cottages behind. It was only when we were around the corner that we burst out laughing.

"Can you believe it? Adams has a girlfriend! Did you see her? She's beautiful. How did he pull that off?" Jack said.

"Hey, he's still my cat. He's handsome, he could get a girl like that," I said, laughing. We kept walking up behind the mansion and then I realized I was in fact leading Jack towards my so-called lair. I guess now that he knew I had one I might as well show it to him.

"Okay, so I'll show you the lair but please remember that I'm your girlfriend and you love me, and that I am not crazy, even though it looks *crazy*," I said. We came up to the cottage and I opened it and Jack followed me in. There was the wall of crazy in all its convoluted glory, the desk with Juliet's journal sitting on top of it.

"Wow, this is crazy," Jack said, looking at the wall. We only stood there for a minute before he grabbed my hand and pulled me outside, closing the door behind him.

"Let's not worry about that stuff right now. I think we should just enjoy ourselves and sit out here on the grass until

Adams' date is over," Jack said and then we started laughing again at the idea of two cats on a date. He was walking down the hill toward a patch of sunlight that was shining through the trees when he kicked a stone and then turned around to face me with a grin.

"Okay, excellent, I'm very impressed with your witch powers. Well done, you got me," he said.

"What are you talking about?"

"This stone here. It even looks old, bravo," he said. I walked over to where he was standing. There, sticking out of the ground was one of the cobblestones much like the one I'd found that had the word 'Lost' inscribed on it. This one had something different. It said 'Jack'.

"Oh and there's another one - 'Took' - and one more - 'Witch'." Jack turned towards me with a smile.

"Jack took witch. Are there meant to be more? Jack took witch to get ice cream? Jack took witch to get married?" he said. He was grinning at me thinking it was some enormous joke that I was playing on him, but all I could feel was icy cold running down my spine, seeming to freeze the blood in my veins.

"There's another one I found that said 'Lost' on it. It's not me doing this," I said.

"So what is it meant to say?" Jack said, confused. "Jack took witch lost?"

The day was sunny, birds chirping in the trees and some butterflies fluttering around but the glacial cold that had taken hold of me crept up my body and constricted my throat. I could barely whisper the words that had rearranged themselves in my mind.

Lost Witch Took Jack.

AUTHOR NOTE

Read Cozy Witch (Torrent Witches #8) now!

Thanks for reading my book! More witch stories to come. If you'd like an email when a new book is released then you can sign up for my mailing list. I have a strict no spam policy and will only send an email when I have a new release.

I hope you enjoyed my work! If you have time, please write a review. They make all the difference to indie Authors.

In the next book authors descend on Harlot Bay like a plague...

xx Tess

TessLake.com